HEIRLOOMS

HEIRLOOMS

Rachel Hall

Winner of the G.S. Sharat Chandra Prize for Short Fiction
Selected by Marge Piercy

BkMk Press
University of Missouri-Kansas City
www.umkc.edu/bkmk

BkMk Press
University of Missouri-Kansas City
5101 Rockhill Road
Kansas City, Missouri 64110
www.umkc.edu/bkmk

Executive Editor: Robert Stewart
Managing Editor: Ben Furnish
Assistant Managing Editor: Cynthia Beard
Author photo: Pamela Frame
French language consultation: Aline de Boton Kultgen

BkMk Press wishes to thank Colleen Boyd, Anders Carlson,
René Ferguson, Abigail Osgood, Lindsey Weishar,
and to Sarah Abrevaya Stein, Julia Phillips Cohen, and
David M. Bunis for Ladino advice.

The G.S. Sharat Chandra Prize wishes to thank Valerie Fioravanti,
Leslie Koffler, Linda Rodriguez, Laura Maylene Walter,
Evan Morgan Williams.

Cover image Gouache "Leben? oder Theater?"
Collection Jewish Historical Museum, Amsterdam.
© Charlotte Salomon Foundation
Charlotte Salomon®
www.jck.nl

Library of Congress Cataloging-in-Publication Data

Names: Hall, Rachel, author.
Title: Heirlooms : stories / Rachel Hall.
Description: Kansas City, Missouri : BkMk Press at the University of
  Missouri-Kansas City, 2016.
Identifiers: LCCN 2016023834 | ISBN 9781886157910 (paperback)
Subjects: LCSH: Jewish families--Fiction. | World War, 1939-1945--Fiction. |
BISAC: FICTION / General. | GSAFD: Historical fiction. | Short stories. |
  War stories.
Classification: LCC PS3608.A5479 A6 2016 | DDC 813/.6--dc23 LC
record available at https://lccn.loc.gov/2016023834

ISBN 978-1-886157-91-0

Acknowledgments

In slightly different forms these stories appeared previously in the following journals: "Saint-Malo, 1940" in *Gettysburg Review*; "La Pousette" in *Lilith*; "Generations" in *Fifth Wednesday*; "Heirlooms" and "In the Cemeteries of Saint-Malo" in *Water~Stone*; "Block Party" in *Bellingham Review*; "Jews of the Middle West" in *Midwestern Gothic.* "White Lies" in *New Letters* and "The War Ends Many Times" in *Natural Bridge.*

My deepest gratitude to everyone who helped bring this book to life.

Thank you to Marge Piercy for selecting my manuscript for the G.S. Sharat Chandra Prize and to the hardworking and talented team at BkMk Press. Thank you to the editors who first published these stories: Brenda Miller and Lee Olson, Sheila O'Connor and Mary Francois Rockcastle, Yona Zeldis McDonough, Vern Miller, Robert James Russell and Jeff Pfaller, Peter Stitt and Mark Drew, Robert Stewart and Dusty Freund. Thanks to Gail Hochman for believing in this book.

Thank you to my colleagues in the English department at Geneseo and to the Geneseo Foundation, which provided funding for the research and writing of this book. Thanks also to the librarians at Geneseo's Milne Library, especially Sue Ann Brainard.

Portions of the book were written at Ragdale and the Ox-Bow School of the Arts, and I am forever grateful for the time and space provided, as well as for the opportunity to work alongside so many wonderful writers and artists: Judith Brotman, Andrea Fritsch, Patrick Creland, Wendy Bilen, Heidi Jensen, Alice Pixley-Young, Ilesa Duncan, Julia Staples, Gail Dodge, Julia Gartrell. Many thanks, too, to the Saltonstall Foundation for the Arts for support and endorsement at a critical juncture.

These stories have benefitted from numerous readers over the years. I am especially grateful to these smart friends for their generosity and insight: Carolyn Alessio, Mary Cantrell, Erika

Dreifus, Kristen Gentry, Julia Green, Maria Lima, Ashley Pankratz, Diane Simmons, and Susan Tekulve.

Thank you to Louise and Burch Craig, Jon Baldo and Roberta Schwartz, Rob Doggett, Gwen Langland, Anna Leahy, Sarah Maxwell, Leslie Pietrzyk, Anne-Marie Reynolds, Sejal Shah, Sarah Webb, Louise Wagner, and Gabi Zolla for sustaining friendships. And thanks to Sheila Cummings for her steadying wisdom.

To my teachers over the years and especially to Robin Metz for letting one more student into his class. And to my students at Geneseo who have enriched my life in numerous ways and have taught me more than they know.

Love and thanks to my sprawling, complex family—especially my brother Daniel and his family: Cindy Eberting Hall, Elly, Kate and Keaton. Thank you also to David and Mary Anne Chazan, superb hosts and tour guides, Dahlia Chazan, Shoshana Chazan, Leli Binstock, and Tali Ben Shabat for her help sorting through old letters in multiple languages, Daniel Chazan for translating and sharing his mother's girlhood diary. To my father Peter Hall, fellow writer, for support and encouragement from the very beginning—and for understanding even when my stories cut close to the bone. And special thanks to my mother, Aline de Boton Kultgen, muse, research assistant, translator, champion. She is everywhere in this book—and in my heart. Thanks also to Jack Kultgen, who came to this party late but has made it so much better.

To Bill for moral and technical support—and so much more. I couldn't have done any of this without you.

And finally, thank you to my daughter Maude, whose coming nudged these stories forth.

For my parents

and

in memory of

Alice and Robert de Boton

סי לוס אניאוס קאלייירון, לוס דידוס קידארון.

Si los aniyos kayeron, los dedos kedaron.

If the rings fall off, the fingers remain.

—Ladino proverb

CONTENTS

SAINT-MALO, 1940

LISE REFOLDS THE NEWSPAPER on the train seat next to her. All week there has been bad news of the war and nothing to do but wait for more. And then this morning the cable: "Come immediately. Esther dying." It is a relief, oddly, to have this task, this errand Lise can accomplish. She has felt this at work, too, engraving invitations. The rote gestures are soothing, the crisp letters satisfying. Even with the war upon them, people are having parties—weddings, anniversaries, baptisms—and Lise is grateful for all these *fêtes*, which seem to her neither foolish nor extravagant.

The train is slowing now and she reaches for the scuffed valise by her feet. It is nearly empty, just a blouse and fresh undergarments for the return trip, and a bar of soap which thuds inside her bag as the train lurches to a stop. She will fill the bag with the baby's things—blankets, sweaters, smocks, and bloomers—made by her sister-in-law. Lise has a memory of Esther sewing tiny, even stitches in the glow of a table lamp, her belly wide, her face flushed. Alain, Lise's twin, had looked on proudly from the settee, and Lise had tried hard not to feel her extraneousness then, her flat stomach, her empty, still hands. Silly to think of that now, she tells herself, rising. She hopes there are plenty of things for Eugénie because money is tight with her own husband at war. She doesn't worry about how she will feed the baby; instead she imagines Eugénie's floaty, dark curls, her solid warmth against her own chest.

This image pulls her through the crowd at the train station, through soldiers locked in embraces with girlfriends or wives, children waving and crying, the vendors selling sandwiches and beer, whole families dressed in holiday clothes, striped parasols in their arms, desperate for distraction. She has forgotten that Saint-Malo is a holiday town, after all. She'd visited here long ago, walked the beach at low tide and then later watched the waves smacking the ramparts, completely covering where she had walked.

It is a perfect day for the beach, she sees, stepping outside. The sky is bright blue, streaked with wispy clouds. She finds a taxi easily, shows the driver the slip of paper with the address—72 rue Godard. She is unwilling to speak, to open herself to a conversation about the weather or the war, for that is all anybody seems to talk about any more. The cab bounces over narrow, cobblestone streets, past the reaching shadow of Cathédrale Saint-Vincent, and halts before a stone apartment building.

"*Merci*," Lise says, paying. She gathers her bag and steps out. She is thinking of another visit before Esther and Alain left Paris, and long before the men were called up. It seems like decades ago, but really it is only two years. When she had entered the apartment, she found Alain and Esther discussing abortion. Lise screamed and cried, begging them to stop. "Lise," her brother had said, "surely you understand this is not a good time for a child." But she had kept on until finally they agreed to have the child. Esther had splashed water on her face. Perhaps she was relieved, too, but they never—any of them—spoke of this again. Instead their letters requesting sponsorship from Jean's friend in America were amended to include the child. Because they all knew it was a bad time, of course they did.

Today the curtains are drawn tight against the midday sun. Lise can't decide if she should ring the buzzer. Finally, she raps on the heavy door. It opens and the nurse squints out at her.

"She's resting now, Madame, but you can go in."

"Thank you," Lise says, setting down her bag with a clatter.

"Hush," the nurse says. "The baby is sleeping, and I can't have you waking her—it's impossible to get her down. She keeps calling for her mother."

"Pardon me," Lise says.

The nurse gestures towards the back of the apartment. "Go ahead," she says, gathering her crocheting from her seat.

Esther is in a dark back bedroom. It smells like ammonia, Lise notes. The nurse has been efficient, if not gentle. The bookshelves by the bed are lined with vials, brown bottles stuffed with cotton and pills, tinctures and salves. There is a photograph of Alain in his uniform propped against the window. How will she recount all this for him? She must remember to tell him of the photograph, the nurse's attention to cleanliness—should she say there were flowers in a vase? A salty breeze from the ocean?

Esther is very still, her body like a child's, curled under a thin blanket. Her breathing is so shallow, that for a moment Lise thinks she is already gone. She settles on a chair and waits—for what? she wonders. In the silence it is hard not to think of all she likes to forget. In particular, her own inability to become pregnant, though Jean is relentless. He doesn't know about her past—the lover who left her, her clandestine abortion, or how she angered the doctor by saying *abortion* too loudly as she was wheeled away. She'd been afraid, a foreigner, a girl with a limp. "I could lose my position, you know," the doctor had hissed.

ESTHER'S SHRIEKS DON'T BUILD in intensity; they simply begin loudly. Lise has goose bumps before she can get to her feet.

"I don't want to die," Esther screams. "I don't want to die!"

Her grip on Lise's arm is strong—too strong for a woman who is dying, Lise finds herself thinking. Up close she notices Esther's clammy smell—yeasty, ripe, too sweet.

"It's okay," Lise says because she has to say something. "It's okay."

Esther's eyes narrow. She seems to know exactly to whom she is speaking. "Fool," she says. Her voice is muffled, as if she has eaten some cotton from the medicine jars. And then again more clearly: "Fool." She rolls over so Lise can see only her matted dark hair, her shoulders under her thin gown. Before Lise has finished feeling the slap of these words, she knows she will never tell anyone about this. What Esther has said hurts because it is true; she is foolish. But she is going to live, and Esther—smart, competent, lovely Esther—is dying before her eyes. She will be dead before Lise can forgive her.

Esther calls out for her mother who is far away in Latvia, whom Esther hasn't seen since she left at sixteen. Lise takes Esther's hand, strokes her forehead. It's Lise, she almost says, still stung, and then thinks better of it. "I'm here, *ma petite*," she says, "I am here with you." We are children in the end, Lise thinks. Frightened, needy children.

When it is over, Lise calls in the nurse to record the time of death. As the nurse checks for a pulse, she clucks her tongue as if Esther hasn't had the good sense to go on living. "*La pauvre*," she says, and Lise wonders who she means. Lise watches her move about the room, snapping open the shades and lifting windows. A sharp light floods the room. Blinking, Lise rises and moves to the armoire. When she opens its doors, Esther's smell—lavender and orange—wafts over her, so she can only stand there for a moment, staring at the neatly folded linens,

Esther's tufted sewing box, the empty shelf where Alain's things should be. Why does she think then of her own messy shelves and drawers, of what Esther would think of the disorder? *Foolish.* Lise takes Esther's navy crêpe dress from the hanger and lays it over the chair. She fingers the lacy inset by the neck, its creamy swirls. Alain has instructed her to buy a good coffin. Eventually, he plans to move Esther to the Jewish cemetery in Paris, but after the war, he will be dead, too, the Jewish cemetery in need of repair. And after a war, so much to consider, so many complications.

From the next room, Lise hears the baby's lilting voice, her musical sounds which become words. "Maman, Maman, Maman," Eugénie sings, her voice growing louder and more purposeful. Lise enters the room. "Maman," Eugénie says and beams when she sees Lise, though Lise looks nothing like Esther. Lise is stout and fair and freckled, will spend the rest of the war zigzagging through her adopted country, Marseille, Le Puy, Lyon, where everyone will think her a Protestant from the North. "Maman," Eugénie says again, reaching up to Lise with dimpled arms.

This, Lise will tell Alain and their family in Palestine, and anyone else who asks. She will tell this story to Eugénie, too, when she is old enough. As she bends to pick up Eugénie, Lise is crying. She has always wanted this baby, always thought that she was hers, and now she is. How horrible she feels, how glad.

LEAVING THE OCCUPIED ZONE

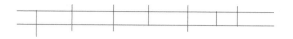

WHILE THE FAITHFUL AND obedient of Montpon-sur-l'Isle kneel and pray, the signs go up. On lampposts, the sides of buildings, store fronts, the *lycée*, and abundantly on the wooden fence protecting the construction of the new lending library. It is a windy day in September, but they've been put up expertly—straight and smooth against the glass or bricks—and don't blow about. The tailor Monsieur Richard, who has missed Mass probably because of his chronic toothache, must see the signs as he hurries into the druggist's. He doesn't see Lise and the pram stopped before one of the signs on rue du Bois. If he did, he isn't likely to think too much of it. Lise suspects that if asked he'd say, "She's Jean's wife, what do I care if she's a Jew?" Though Jean is plenty proud of this fact. He'd told everyone when he announced his marriage. "A Jewess from Palestine! A beautiful Jewess." Lise had hushed him, embarrassed, but not yet aware of the way her background might be better kept close. Lise is fair and freckled and speaks perfect, accentless French. The child, it is true, is darker, but people always comment how much she looks like Jean. And wisely, he hasn't disabused them of this notion.

The signs indicate that all Jews must register at City Hall within the next forty-eight hours. There are penalties for those who are not prompt and severe punishment for those who ignore this decree. Lise feels her face heat as if she's done something base before a crowd.

She has gone out this morning with the stroller because the child was fussy—sleepy but unable to fall asleep, overtired perhaps. Soothing her into quiet had consumed the entirety of Lise's thoughts. The fresh air and the rocking rhythm of the pram had done the trick as Lise had hoped they would. The relief was still fresh, when she stopped before the sign.

The church bells toll, issuing in the new hour, the end of weekday Mass. She usually finds the sound pleasing, something majestic and yearning in the timbre. Now, though, the sound is jarring, a voice raised in anger. She turns toward home, thinking as she steers around divots and potholes, what is necessary to pack. Money, papers, layers of clothing.

These items she is throwing into her knapsack when Mother returns from Mass, the shawl around her shoulders carrying in the incense smell of the church. "What is happening?" she asks. Her blue eyes, so much like Jean's, take in the piles, the knapsack.

Lise is so far along the path of her departure that she is surprised to find Mother hasn't accompanied her. She's staring at her as she digs through drawers, gathers diapers.

"Did you not see them?"

"Tell me what you are talking about."

Lise explains, not stopping her sorting and packing.

"You're going without Jean?"

"I can't wait," Lise says. Who knows how long before he's back from the army, though others have returned, stooped, their tails between their legs.

It has been said of Lise, all her life, that she's a dreamer, her head in the clouds, so she is surprised to learn that she knows now what she must do. And without delay.

"The child can stay with me."

Lise stops packing. "All Jews, the sign said, regardless of age." Even if the signs were less clear, Lise cannot part from the child's steadying warmth, the fierce call of her needs—milk, sleep, song. "She comes with me, naturally."

"I have some valerian from the pharmacy," Mother says. "It will keep her quiet for the trip."

She moves then into the kitchen, and Lise can hear her gathering food for the journey. Lise remembers the envelope of francs beneath the mattress. She extracts it, puts some in her pocket and some deep in the knapsack.

In the kitchen, Mother has a bundle of food packed up. It's too big, Lise worries, but she accepts it. "Coats," she says, and then we're off."

"Take this," Mother says, tugging a gold ring from her hand. Lise knows it was her mother's.

"I couldn't," Lise protests.

"You'll bring it back if you don't need it," Mother says. She turns to gather the coats.

Lise tries again, but Mother turns, thrusts her coat at her.

"I feel rain coming," she says. "Hurry."

Lise slips the ring on her finger above her wedding band. "Thank you, Mother," she says. Though she has opened her home to Lise and the child, Lise hasn't known what her mother-in-law felt about her. She imagines that her mother-in-law might have liked Jean to marry one of the local girls, a Catholic like herself. Certainly that would be easier for everyone. But now she has her mother's ring, and Mother is taking her own coat from the closet. "Come," she says. "We'll take a midday walk to visit the Derains."

Gratitude floods her. And respect—for this is an excellent idea. She can't speak. How often they have walked together, passing the neighbors, friends who tousle Eugénie's curls, comment on her growth.

The child sleeps on, miraculously, in her stroller. Mother takes Lise's arm in hers and they set out, as if for a leisurely walk. They pass the neighbors' well-tended houses, the geraniums in their window boxes holding out against the cold. A pair of shutters creaks shut above them. Inside, families are sitting down to their midday meal. Indeed, Lise can smell someone's roast cooking with rosemary. They pass the *pâtisserie*, closed midday. The striped awning flaps in the wind. They pass the *lycée*, quiet at this hour, too. Without discussing it, they veer north here, avoiding the municipal building. Are there lines forming already? Are there police? Dogs? She can't think of it.

Then they are at the Derains and she lifts Eugénie from the stroller. Mother takes it, pulls the blankets up and pulls the hood low. They haven't seen any police so far. Perhaps they, too, are finishing dinner, resting, their hands folded over happy bellies.

"Past the orchard, there are woods. Cross the stream and keep going to the road," Mother says. "It's two kilometers at most."

Lise knows she is lucky that Mother knows this area, played in these fields as a girl, picnicked in the woods as a young woman. And yet, lucky isn't quite the right word for her situation. "Go on," Mother says. She has turned before Lise can embrace her or whisper her thanks.

Lise's bag is tucked under her coat. The child is on her hip, heavy and warm. Already Lise is sweating in her layers. If she is stopped, she will say she's come looking for apples for sauce. "The Derains have always allowed me to pick here," she'll say. One can expect some sloppiness and confusion about the new rules. But the orchard is quiet, empty except for the wind through the leaves. The ground is strewn with rotting apples and bees buzzing drunkenly.

At the end of the row, she steps into the woods. Beneath her feet, rocks crunch. It's cooler here, but her hip hurts. Even with the extra heel on her right shoe, the old pain returns. If she slows, the noise seems even louder. The birds squawk at her, chiding, *go, go, go*. She feels her heart whirring in her chest. The child nestles her head into Lise's neck. Her eyes are open, but glazed from the herb. Not too much, she hopes. Could that be the road already? She thinks she hears the clomp of horses. Perhaps she can catch a ride to town. Her hip under the child has begun to throb in its familiar way. She tries to shift Eugénie but she lets out a whimper. It's not worth it. "We're almost there, my flower."

She comes to a thin ribbon of a stream. On either side there are ferns as big as bushes. She'd like to drink, to splash water on her face, but she can't stop.

"Hold it, there." A policeman steps from behind a bush, pointing a gun at her.

He's French, she notes. The brown uniform looks brand new, crisply pressed.

"Where are you going?"

"To Clermont. My husband's unit has been demobilized there." Perhaps this fellow was also at the Line, will sympathize.

"This is forbidden."

The policeman is young, she sees; his face is splotched with angry purple bumps. "To see my husband?"

"Don't be stupid."

"I must get to him. He's injured."

"It will cost you," the policeman says. He squints into the distance.

"Take this," Lise says, pulling the rings from her finger. "For your sweetheart."

His eyes narrow, as if accustomed to ridicule. He takes the rings without looking, slips them in his jacket pocket and buttons the flap. "Put the child there," he says. He points to a tarp and his canteen behind the bush. From his side pocket, he extracts a set of keys. He tosses them onto the tarp. "The little ones love keys," he says.

Lise doesn't have time to wonder how he has gleaned this bit of domestic know-how, because he is yanking her to the ground, stuffing his tongue into her mouth. He tastes improbably of porridge. She tries not to gag, but she can't help it.

"You don't like me?" He mocks surprise, but his look is steely.

"It's not that," Lise says.

"Never mind," he says, unzipping his pants. He tugs at her clothing, pulling it out of his way. She shuts her eyes against his ugly pushing. She hears fabric tearing—her wool stockings. She sees behind her closed lids, the ladder-like pattern a tear makes. She thinks of ladders, then, of climbing up. That is what she is doing here, climbing. One step, then another. Hurry, she thinks, hurry, until her mind is filled with just that one word, her ascent.

From the distance, Lise can hear Eugénie beginning to cry. Soon, she'll try to crawl to Lise. "The child," she says. Her voice sounds wooly to her, tentative, as if she were the child.

He says nothing until he's finished with her. Then he stands. "Hurry up," he says.

Lise scrambles, trying to do everything at once—stand, grab for the child, put distance between herself and this brute. Instead she falls back on her bad hip.

"Clumsy slut," the soldier says, lighting a cigarette.

Lise tries again, this time more carefully. She collects Eugénie. "No, no, no," Eugénie says, but she's not crying.

Lise adjusts her coat as she runs, not looking back, shame clawing at her. How has she let this happen?

Not far off she sees the road, empty of cars, of police, of carts, for the moment. She crosses, and then she is in the unoccupied zone. She has expected to feel something—relief at least, but in fact, she feels nothing yet, nothing but the throbbing of her hip, the awareness that the child's diaper is in need of changing. "It's ok," Lise says. The child seems to believe her; her muttering has stopped.

IN THE NEXT VILLAGE over, she stops at a café. By the fireplace, a cluster of policemen is playing cards. Their brown jackets make her heart clatter in her chest. She must lean against the wall for a moment. The men hardly look up from their game, but Lise feels her face burning. In the WC, she peels off her torn stockings, the damp underwear. She should rinse it out, save the stockings to mend. She has only this pair. A great luxury, she allows herself then, balling them up and stuffing them into the dustbin. Discarding the whole mess. Her hip is sore, but not yet black and blue. That will come later, she suspects. She cups her hands and fills them with water, cleaning herself as best she can. Eugénie laughs at her efforts, the water splashing onto the dirty tile floor. The laugh surprises Lise. It tinkles out, echoes in the dank little room.

The café is filling up for dinner, but she finds a spot at the bar. For a moment she imagines Jean grinning, bragging about his Jewess. He couldn't have known, and still, there is this hard fact, like a pebble in her shoe: If he'd said nothing, she'd be in Montpon still, clearing supper dishes perhaps, taking out her knitting.

She and Eugénie eat a bowl of vegetable soup. Lise hardly tastes it, but the heat is pleasant. She is happy to see that the child's appetite is fine, despite her continued drowsiness. The waitress tells her it is five kilometers to the train station.

"The Shuwers are heading that direction," she says, pointing towards the next table. A man in a rumpled jacket is hunched over his plate, his back to her. The woman with him is plump with a shiny red face.

A ride is procured for a couple of francs. Lise calculates that she has enough for train tickets and some food for the journey still. The rings. How foolish to have offered them up unnecessarily. Her head is filling with regret and reproach, treacherous thoughts to be avoided, her own forbidden zones. Like her thoughts about Jean's bragging, these thoughts must be avoided.

The farmer opens the back door of his car for her. There is an old blanket covering the seat and when she sits, she understands why. The springs jab at her. She pulls Eugénie onto her lap. As they back out of the parking area, gravel pings the underbelly of the car.

"The child is well-behaved," the woman says. Her first words to Lise. "Mine were too."

"Except when they weren't," the farmer says, laughing at his joke. "Where you headed to from here?"

"Tulle," Lise says, quickly. "My mother is in the hospital."

"Garlic," the woman says.

"I beg your pardon?"

"It's good for the organs," the woman says.

Lise realizes then that the truck is redolent with the bite of garlic. "I will make sure she gets some," Lise says.

Out the window, Lise sees a sign indicating the direction to Montpon. It is only five kilometers away, but that hardly seems possible.

THE TRAIN STATION IS crowded and smells of cigarettes and woolens pulled from storage. There are still groups of soldiers returning from the front, families heading south, as she is. Like ants, Lise thinks, swarming from their hill, and she is one of them. Slowing to consider the ticket lines, her fear flares up. No, she must keep moving. She decides to buy her ticket on board, though it will cost a bit more. There is something calming—or maybe just distracting—in action. She thinks of her mother-in-law and her rosary, her lips and hands moving.

She is able to find a seat in a cabin with a student, a young man, bent over his text. He looks up with irritation as she sits. Lise tucks the knapsack on the rack above just before the cabin fills with other passengers—a family of four and a gentleman with a large portfolio, which he slips between his seat and the window. Then the train heaves and begins its journey.

It has begun to rain. Lise can hear it now on the roof, a steady beat. "How lucky we are to be inside now, where it is warm and dry," she says to the others. She is aware of something pitiful and necessary about this sifting, scrambling insistence on luck.

"Indeed," says the man near the window.

Montpon-sur-l'Isle is gone, then the whole region, its vineyards and orchards. Her plan up until this point has been to get out of Montpon. She has done that, but now what? Now what? The train's clattering over the tracks seems to demand an answer from her. She can't think with all the noise and activity in the compartment and she can't leave either. Not without losing her seat. Her hip aches.

In the end she purchases a ticket for Marseille, as far as she can get from the Occupied Zone. If nothing else, there is the sea, the one she knows from her girlhood, from Jaffa. She tries to imagine the water now, the heat of home, but her memories are slippery, not something she can hold onto.

The next station is so crowded that Lise cannot make out the name of the town. People crowd on, filling even the aisle outside their compartment. Someone says that the WC is occupied in this manner as well. Through the window, Lise can see the people seated on their valises, bundles on their backs. She feels packed in, stuffed and surrounded.

The effects of the valerian have worn off and Eugénie wants attention. Lise makes her fingers into dancing girls, she sings softly. She tells her stories and bounces her on her knee. She wishes for a storybook, but she has brought nothing like that. Near suppertime, she breaks up some bread and the child eats. Lise eats, too, though she isn't hungry. She knows she needs to keep up her strength. She will give Eugénie the other bottle with the valerian later and hope it works again. The family in their compartment has broken out their supper—sausage and a strong cheese. The mother doles out pieces of chocolate to the children. She holds out a piece to Lise, frowning. Her look seems to say that she has planned ahead, and has only so much sympathy for those who have not. "For the child," she says.

"*Merci*," Lise says. "We left in such a rush." And then feels that she's said too much; she is defending herself against the wrong charges. She must be careful.

EUGÉNIE STIRS IN HER sleep. The gentleman with the portfolio is the only other passenger awake. He looks up from the paper before him and nods at her. Though she has wanted quiet to think, it now feels dangerous: she is back in the woods, the damp ground seeping through her skirt. She mustn't go back there. She needs to keep her mind anchored here.

"You're an artist," she says.

"An architect."

"May I see?"

He turns the drawing around and passes it over the snoring student. "It's to be built in Port-de-Bouc."

The paper is a deep blue, neither turquoise nor cobalt, but some blend of the two. The white lines of the drawing are

26

intricate, showing windowpanes, shelving, cornices, moldings, the dimensions marked in small print. There is a wall of windows opening up to the sea. The drawing reminds her of her brother Alain's anatomy books with the clear pages one can pull back to show the muscles and the bones. With both, there is something reassuring and mesmerizing.

"Is this a patio?"

"Yes, with a garden around it." He points to a series of terraced beds.

"Beautiful," Lise says.

"If it gets built at all. Who can say with the present situation?" He shakes his head, looks like he wants to say more.

Lise hands back the drawing.

"And you, Madame, are you an artist?"

"Oh, no. I work at a printers shop." This is only partly untrue. She hasn't painted since Jean and Alain were summoned to the front. She had her supplies in Montpon but hadn't once taken them out, not even her sketchbook. It seems impossible that she will have again that necessary calm and desire.

"You have an artistic bent, nonetheless," the gentleman says. "I can tell by your attention to my work."

"As a girl, perhaps, I dabbled," Lise says.

Eugénie stirs and Lise shifts her to get her comfortable. When she looks up, the man is rubbing the bridge of his nose where his spectacles have left a purple dent.

"You must be staying near the Vieux-Port. That is where all the artists gather. Excellent cafés."

"I'm sure my husband has found a good place," she says.

"Particularly Le Brûleur de Loups Café. Most inviting. Good people."

The young mother opens her eyes and huffs her disapproval.

"Thank you for showing me your drawings," Lise whispers, shifting slightly to face the window, so he won't see how grateful she is, how relieved. A destination. In her mind, she repeats the name of the café.

She must've slept, because it is morning when she looks out the window again. The rain has been left behind with so much else and it is bright, the sun warming her in her seat. When Lise shifts out of the sun, Eugénie awakens. "Maman," she says crossly. At her crown, her curls are damp. Lise offers her some pear that she bites off for her. There is a little milk left, and the child gulps it down, too.

The architect rises as they near his stop. Lise wishes she could see the drawings again, the soothing velvety blue, the precise lines, but there isn't time and what purpose would it serve?

"Good luck with your project, Monsieur," she says.

"To you as well," he says.

At the door to the compartment, he turns. "Remember Le Brûleur de Loups Café." And then he is gone, the drawings—with their care to detail and promise of order—with him.

In Marseille, the train empties out. The corridor outside their compartment is littered with bent cigarette butts, paper wrappers, newspapers splayed open—things used and discarded, stepped on in the rush. The squalor fills her with a swirling shame, and she must lean for a moment against a bench. She thinks of her ruined wool stockings, coiled in the trash bin near Montpon. But that is silly, she tells herself. It will get cleaned up. Of course it will. Already men with long-handled dustbins and brooms wait at the doors to begin their work.

She follows the crowd out of the station and into a busy square. There are signs on posts pointing in all directions—the market, the beach, the old harbor. She takes the main street in the direction of the harbor. She will locate the café the architect mentioned, and then what? Think, she chides herself. All the way to the harbor, she asks herself the same question. She is thinking too hard on the subject. The concentration is yielding nothing. Better to step back, look away and an answer will come. She steps off the main street onto a narrow side street. Wash flaps on a clothesline above her head. It's quiet here, as if the inhabitants are waiting for the sun to mount the tall buildings and rouse them.

There by a small square is the café the architect mentioned. A red awning juts out over several wicker tables and chairs. There is a fat calico sunning itself on the front step. It looks fine, the café, a bit shabby perhaps.

"We'll go see the water," she tells the child, to fill the silence. "How would you like that?" Her voice warbles.

At the beach, Lise takes off Eugénie's shoes, then her own. The sand hasn't yet warmed, and it squishes damp and cool between her toes. They wade in and let the water wash over their feet. Eugénie stomps and kicks, laughing at the splashes. In the distance, Lise can see the brightly painted boats bobbing. The water stretches out before her—blue-green, then silvery, then gray. Beyond that is Algiers, she knows. It may be better there, safer. She is surprised to discover that it is harder than one might guess to end a journey such as this. There is something insistent and fluttery inside, urging her on.

Near a grassy area, there are benches and fountains for rinsing the sand from their feet. She dries the child's feet with her skirt, tickling her so she squirms.

"Now that we've bathed, we will have breakfast," she tells the child. Inside, it smells of burnt sugar and coffee and Lise realizes she is hungry. Similarly, when she sits, she feels her fatigue. The coffee is good and strong and it clears her head. The child gobbles the bread Lise spreads with jam.

When the bill arrives, Lise is shocked by the total. "Big city prices," the waitress says, not unkindly. And she points Lise to a board by the WC where rooms for let are posted. Again, the prices are alarming. Judging from the address, one room is nearby. This is what she will do next. If it's suitable, she will find a way to get rent. An address is crucial for correspondence with Mother, with Jean and Alain. She steps out into the sunshine, feels its warmth on her face.

Someone is calling to her. She squints in the direction of the calls. A small woman, her dark hair pulled back, says again, "Lise, is that you?" She smiles. Lise feels a flood of warmth for the woman before recognition. And then, recognition comes: It is Clara Israel, the wife of Alain's medical-school classmate. They left Paris in June. Of course!

"Come," Clara says, assessing the situation immediately. "You'll stay with us until Jean comes—and Alain, no doubt."

Soon, Lise, too, will recognize those in flight, not from their valises or bulky layers, but by the expression on their wan faces, a look that registers all they've left behind. They will think themselves lucky to have escaped the Occupied Zone, as she does. How can she not, her arm linked with Clara's? She squeezes Clara's arm and follows her, ignoring for now the sea, the sky above Algiers, its beckoning blue.

Later, when Lise tells the story of leaving the Occupied Zone, she will remember her mother-in-law's arm in hers, the kind architect, his meticulous drawings, the way his advice led her to the right place. And then Clara, calling out across the bright plaza. What luck, Lise says. In her telling, she minimizes certain difficulties. The loss of her only pair of wool stockings, for example, she omits altogether. One could almost say that the losses are nearly lost themselves. *Almost. Nearly.*

LA POUSSETTE

SYLVIE BEAUCHARD HAS BEEN cooking since dawn. Now at half-past twelve, she thinks longingly of her bed—the heavy blankets and cool sheets, the dark bedroom tucked away in the eaves. This is a new development, this kind of fatigue—one that she cannot argue with. Her in-laws will be here shortly and this thought awakens her, so that she is brisk and darting in the dining room, snapping down the linens and cutlery. Where is Charles? He will want to open the wine so it can breathe before he fills the glasses. These she places carefully by the plates. The pale green stems make her think of tulips and she wishes she had some for a vase. It is too early for flowers and besides, she chides herself, she has what she has most wished for.

She has planned the exact way to tell Charles' parents about their grandchild. Charles has agreed to her plan, though he'd said he would prefer to tell them straight away. After the meal, Sylvie will suggest they go to the front room for dessert. (The hazelnut torte is indeed the reason for rising before dawn. It has layers and filling and a frosting made glossy and smooth by her hand.) Once seated, she will take out her knitting—a tiny sweater in the palest blue. How long before they notice what she is making? With her father-in-law it could be hours. He'll start in with news of the Occupied Zone, then move on to the price of petrol in Nîmes, but Mother will notice. She will raise her eyebrows, gather her lips, a look Sylvie finds fearsome still, though it is Mother's most common expression. She will demand to know what Sylvie is doing and why. And then they can tell her, watch her impatience and annoyance turn to pleasure, maybe even pride, who knows? But Sylvie has gotten ahead of herself. There is still work to be done before they arrive.

From the window over her sink, Sylvie can see Charles in the orchard, heading back this way. Because she is focused on the tasks before her, she doesn't notice the changing quality of light. It is brighter, sharper, the shadows more pronounced from the still-leafless trees.

The tenants in the next farm over have been out in the orchards, she notices, because they've left buckets and ladders. It had pleased her at first to think of the farm being inhabited again. Then she saw the tenants in town with their city clothes and manners. The woman's skirt had a series of pleats in the back that flipped up prettily when she walked. They weren't farmers, she thought then, and sure enough, Charles had found their cow in his pasture. When he took it back he'd found them reading books. Books about farming! Who knew such a thing existed? Were there also books about walking? he'd asked Sylvie. Taking a leak in the woods? That was weeks ago, and still Sylvie will hear him laughing in the other room and know he's thinking of the neighbors and their books.

And now, here he is, stomping his feet outside the door to get the dirt off them as she has taught him.

"The wine," she says when he is in.

"Yes, yes."

He is not one to be rushed, Sylvie knows, but he wants the dinner to go well, too. A son would make his life easier, but Sylvie cannot help herself; she wants a girl. From the cellar,

Charles retrieves two bottles. He wipes off the dust and mildew with a rag.

"I'm hungry," he says. "Is it ready?"

He's been up for hours, too. Outside the dogs—Sammi and Bruno—bark. Sylvie smiles, thinking how seriously the pups take this job. They are good dogs, loyal and affectionate, fine company when Charles is gone. She has brushed them this morning, so she knows they are sleek as well as graceful as they follow Father Beauchard's truck. Over the barking she can hear the truck sputter and grind on its ascent. Sylvie pats her hair into place, tucks a loose strand behind her ear. There isn't time to change into a fresh apron. Pity.

"*Bienvenue!*" Sylvie calls to her in-laws, "Come in, come in!"

"Please," Mother Beauchard says, "I'm not the Queen, just a tired old woman." She pecks Charles on each cheek. Her fingers grip Sylvie's shoulders as she pulls her in for her kisses. There is nothing frail or failing in her touch, Sylvie thinks.

"Where is Papa?" Charles asks, taking her coat and kerchief.

"With your beasts," she says. "He brought them bones."

"He's sweet on those two," Charles says.

"Humpf," says Mother. "Just two more mouths to feed, that's all they are."

Sylvie knows where this conversation is going. They've heard it a dozen times: they spoil the dogs, treat them like children. If they had children they'd see how foolish they look.

"That yarn is lovely," Sylvie says, reaching for Mother's arm in a new sweater.

"I should assume so," Mother says. "I traded plenty for the wool."

"It's a good color on you."

"What does an old woman care for color?" Mother says, but Sylvie can tell she is pleased. She puffs up like the tawny *poule* before she lays.

Father Beauchard has been drinking already, Sylvie sees when he enters. It is his right, Charles would say. He works every day and is entitled to a good drunk if he wants one. He's mild and affectionate when he drinks, no trouble. He might grow mushy at their news, but that isn't a crime, not at all.

"Father," she says kissing him. She smells the wine on his breath—warm and briny against her cheek.

"Shall we sit down?"

"Yes, please."

"It's not yet Easter," Mother says, taking in the tablecloth, the good glasses. "Such fuss for family."

"Never mind," says Father. "Never mind."

Charles tries to catch her eye. He'd like to blurt their news, to stave off his mother's relentless crabbing, but Sylvie won't look. She must get the roast from the stovetop where it cools. The juices will make a good gravy, thickened just a bit with flour, a touch of wine. Then the dogs bark again.

"Such a nuisance," Mother says, pleased, her view confirmed.

There is a rap at the door and through the kitchen window, Sylvie sees it is the neighbors. All over the village, families are sitting down to Sunday supper. What can they possibly want at this time? Father is liable to invite them in, tell them the history of this house, the village. His favorite is the story about their region being the model for Heaven, such is its charm. Between her mother-in-law's sourness and this interruption, Sylvie's high hopes for the day falter and then plummet.

She opens the door. "*Oui?*" Two men stand before her, their dark round spectacles making their eyes look particularly inquisitive. With them is the woman in her pleated skirt. This time she pushes a stylish *poussette*, and in it, a little girl with wispy dark curls, the kind Sylvie would like to smooth with her hand. Sharply, the child turns her head from Sylvie's gaze.

"Good afternoon," the taller man says. His dark hair is brushed back from a high forehead. "We're your neighbors from down the way." Sylvie catches a whiff of something foreign in his speech.

"*Oui*," Sylvie says again.

"We were hoping to speak with you regarding—"

But then Father Beauchard, gregarious with wine, calls from the other room, "Come in! *Bienvenue!*" Sylvie opens the door wider, so they can all enter. The shorter man lifts the carriage over the stone threshold, and then the child is removed. She goes to the woman, tugs on her skirt to be lifted. Once on her hip, she buries her face in the woman's shoulder. In the past, such a display would've pained Sylvie.

"We've interrupted you," the woman says, seeing the table, the open bottle of wine. "We'll not bother you long."

"No bother, no bother," says Charles.

"We must inquire," says the shorter man. "If you have any food you would sell. You see, the farm isn't yet producing."

"No," says Sylvie, before Charles can answer. She wants them to leave *tout de suite* so she can resume her cooking, proceed to the announcement, the celebratory cake. Yes, a plan is a good thing and ought not to be deviated from once established.

Mother Beauchard looks surprised at her answer, but she knows as well as Sylvie that one must stock up for the tough times to come. Perhaps she is annoyed that Sylvie spoke before Charles. Sylvie isn't sure, but it is pleasing to have surprised her mother-in-law, who clearly dislikes the sensation. Sylvie doesn't care for surprises either, which is why it is now critical that the neighbors leave. She tries to usher them toward the door again. She sees that during this interruption the potatoes have boiled over, leaving starchy ribbons down the side of the big pot.

"Potatoes," says the woman.

"For the pigs," Sylvie says.

35

"Would you consider for the child?" the woman, Lise, says. "She is hungry, growing."

The child has round cheeks, legs like sausages. Even her fingers are pudgy. Is she pale? Perhaps, but it is that time of year. The child stares at her, her dark eyes appraising, it seems.

"We must take care of our own," Sylvie says, averting her eyes.

"You know about the market on Tuesday?" Charles says. "Some will barter there."

Sylvie watches the woman return the child to her stroller. It's an attractive little *poussette* with big wheels, a navy awning and seat with a sturdy basket beneath. She has seen these only in advertisements in magazines. And though there are no sidewalks nearby or gardens or parks in which to push a *poussette*, Sylvie must have it. Why should this baby have one and not hers?

"Wait," she says. "I've forgotten the barley." Neither she nor Charles care for it, not its chewy texture, or its taste. But these people can't be choosy, even with their fancy ways.

"For the *poussette*," she says, "a hundred kilos."

"Ridiculous," says Mother Beauchard. Sylvie hasn't heard her enter the kitchen.

The child is being lifted out in protest, her fat little legs kicking. From under the seat, a blanket and parcel are removed. "*Et voilà,*" says the shorter of the men.

"What do you need with that?" Mother Beauchard says.

Sylvie doesn't care what Mother thinks. She takes the handle, which feels just right in her hands, and steers the *poussette* past her frowning mother-in-law, out of the kitchen smelling of burnt meat and into the front parlor. A little throne, she thinks, parking it before the window. Charles has brought up the barley in its burlap sacks. The men each lift a sack, hoist it on their shoulders and take off down the hill.

36

"I'll bring the rest around after *midi*," Charles says.

"Well," says Father Beauchard, "Where were we?"

"Mother," Sylvie says, cupping her only slightly enlarged belly, "have you not guessed it? We are having a child."

"Bravo!" says her father-in-law. "Congratulations to the both of you—and to us as well—a grandchild!"

When Sylvie looks to Mother Beauchard, she sees that she is smiling. Is it possible that her eyes are even wet? Later, Sylvie will remember this door opening between them, approval like a light shining on her, warming her. This was not her plan, but it has worked out. Even the meat is fine, not over-cooked, as she had feared. They eat well, sopping up the juices with the crusty bread and nearly polishing off the cake.

LISE HASN'T SEEN SUCH plenty since before the war. There'd been fruit compote in a green glass bowl, a fat, golden loaf on the breadboard, meat crackling in the oven, a cake with chocolate frosting, hazelnuts circling the top. She had expected the woman to offer some to Eugénie. How long since the child had had a sweet? Where Lise is from, guests are a blessing. They are ushered in, fed the last morsel, given the best seat at the table.

But Palestine seems not just far away to her; it is from another time, some distant past. There is so much here that her parents would dislike or misunderstand—the young couples walking arm in arm, Lise's own calf-baring skirts, the crisp greetings in the shops and offices down town, greetings which seem at first to welcome but do not, not really.

March 13, 1941

Très chers,

At present, we are living in the Vaucluse region. The farm has cherry orchards and almond trees already established, and we have planted potatoes and wheat. Until then, we have barley,

which our neighbors grow in abundance. Besides crops, we have
chickens and a cow named Mathilde. She is a good cow, so we
have milk for the child and cheese and butter. Eugénie delights in
the space here and grows like a mushroom. Kisses to all of you,
from all of us.
    Lise

OF BARLEY, ONE CAN say this: it is versatile. Lise makes porridge
with it for breakfast. She roasts the kernels and makes a kind
of coffee. Adding the first scraggly vegetables and wild garlic,
she makes soup. She grinds it into flour and makes bread and
cake, adding cherries from the orchard once they ripen. They
don't go hungry, but she will never eat barley again after the
war, won't even consider it. Just the smell of it cooking will
turn her stomach.

By June, Alain and Jean have mapped the property and
have cleared a spot for planes to land. She knows this much,
but not what they will bring or take away—food? Ammunitions?
People? Her brother and husband speak of this after supper
while she cleans, puts Eugénie to bed. So often, she thinks, since
the war began, she can do nothing about what most troubles
her. She cannot solve the most pressing problems, but she can't
bear not to act either, so she cleans the crumbling stone floor,
tidies the shelves. This activity both occupies and distracts,
though not indefinitely, not perfectly.

Sometimes she knits while they talk, counting stitches, rows,
her progress. She hears them but doesn't. This is the other
discovery she makes during this time—the mind can know and
not, hold apart certain facts where they aren't as bothersome.

She is making a cardigan for Eugénie from wool that was
Jean's sweater before he tore the sleeve on a fence. She has
salvaged what she could. It's rough dark yarn, too scratchy for
a child, but it will keep out the cold. Eugénie is a good girl, as

if she knows she mustn't complain. What will be the cost of all this early and necessary compliance, Lise wonders. There is too much to do—the henhouse to clean, the cow to milk—for Lise to consider this long. And then her brother is gone to Lyon where he does God knows what. Each time he returns she is afraid it will be the last time she sees him. He and Jean speak late into the night, and she cannot bear their murmurs.

WHEN IT HAPPENS, CHARLES has gone to the mill in Avignon. Sylvie is in the pantry gathering ingredients for a tart when a cramp seizes her, a knife between her legs, so sharp that she clutches herself there, that place she knows only as *down there*. Through the layers of dress and apron, wool stockings, she feels the dampness. It's too early for this. Too soon. *Pas encore*, she whispers, as if hushing a baby back to sleep. *Pas encore*. She cannot remember when she last felt the baby moving inside her—was it last night? This morning before the milking? Then she can think of nothing but the hot, rude pain.

When Charles returns, it is all over. The blood and mess have been disposed of, the floor mopped clean. He comes home smelling of wheat and wine and is slow to understand when Sylvie tells him the baby is gone.

As SOON AS HE entered, the doctor gave her a tablet to swallow. She would like to sleep for a long time, but after the examination, the doctor insists on talking to her. Charles, in his muddy work boots, stands by the bed. When he leaves, there will be two discrete piles of dirt on the bedroom floor.

"The womb," the doctor says, "is a vessel." He picks up the glass beside the bed to illustrate. "Yours is tilted, Madame. Like this."

Sylvie turns her head into the pillow. The bedding smells sour to her, unfresh.

"I know this is not what you want to hear," he says. "But you must accept, Madame."

Sylvie can hear Charles shuffling, grinding the dirt into her floor. So much mess, she thinks.

"I recommend rest," the doctor says, "and quiet."

"Yes, yes, of course," Charles says.

"There is a neighbor girl who can help out?"

"My mother will come," Charles says.

Sylvie keeps her face in the pillow even after she hears the door click shut behind them. She hears their voices in the next room, but the words seem not to adhere one to another, they are separated by vast gulfs. Then it is quiet. A breeze comes through the open window, ruffles the leaves.

HOW MANY DAYS PASS in this manner? Tea and bread, then sleep. Soup and more sleep. One day after the bleeding has at last stopped, she feels well enough to sit up and knit, but the discovery of the small yellow bonnet, nearly completed on her needles, sets her back. Should she continue? Or unravel all her hard work? The yarn is good cotton, but what to do with it, she cannot imagine. She sets it on the pillow beside her, lies back down. Then from the window, happy shrieking, peals of laughter. It's the girl with the dark curls. Sylvie rises and goes to the window. She can see the child running from one of the men, laughing. The man sings as he scoops her up, and she shrieks again. Sylvie shuts the window, pulls closed the curtain. Still the noise seeps in: piercing, ruinous. She knows what she must do. Hasn't the doctor insisted on quiet?

At Hôtel de Ville, Sylvie is made timid by the lines and movement, the brisk efficiency of high heels clacking over the tiled floor and the voices echoing up into the high ceiling. The entry way smells of rain and cigarettes. Thank goodness, there is a placard by the entrance that directs her where she needs to go. What will she say to Monsieur Gilbert? How does she know they are Jews? Their speech, the dark hair, spectacles—don't Jews always have poor eyesight?

As it turns out, she needn't have proof. Any suspicion in this time is sufficient. Monsieur Gilbert thanks her and moves her quickly along. He'd rather spend his time practicing *boule* than worrying about Jews, but there is pressure from Paris. Still, he thinks, he will play his match after lunch as he intended, before sending out the gendarmes.

MID-MORNING, WHILE LISE KNITS, there is a knock at the door. This could be any number of things—the cow in the neighbors' field again, or a peddler, but Lise knows it is something more. She watches Jean at the door, combing his hair back with his hand as he listens. The man who has been sent to warn them is no one she knows, but that is to be expected. "You must hurry," he says. Before the door is closed, she is gathering their things—clothes, books, papers. A sack of barley cakes and the first almonds from the trees. They're on a train to Lyon before dark.

August 12, 1941

Bien chers tous,

> *By the time you read this, we will be in our new town. Alain promises it is a good place, and you know how he is always right about such things. Jean will find work in a lab. Alain assures us of this as well. I imagine there will be parks for Eugénie with paths we can wander.*

She stops writing for a moment, remembering the stroller. Is it growing easier, this leaving and discarding? She cannot even remember all she has left or abandoned, so it's funny that she will remember the stroller for a long time. Beside her, Eugénie sleeps, her cloth doll in her arms. Lise leans her forehead against the glass. In the last light, the fields outside gleam. She must finish her letter, so she can post it at the next station. There is much she cannot write her parents and her sister Allegra about: not the roundups in Paris, for instance, not her new awareness of the gradations and varieties of fear—one that numbs, another that makes her sharp and quick, certainly not Alain's and Jean's involvement with the Resistance.

> *We are passing through the ochre hills, as I write. I hope I can remember their particular yellow, as well as the fields of lavender and mustard.*
>
> *Perhaps when you read this, we will be sitting down to supper in our new apartment. Our new place will be smaller than the farm, but city living is like that. Think of us there—safe and together and missing you.*
>
> *Lise*

When Charles mentions the neighbors' sudden departure, Sylvie shrugs, continues her polishing. She tells no one what she has done—not Charles or her in-laws. All that warm fall when she opens the windows, she imagines she hears the girl calling out or singing. But no, it's only the wind sifting through the leaves on the larch trees, and farther off, Charles cutting hay.

THE BABY CARRIAGE AND the layette of gowns and sweaters she'd assembled were taken away while she convalesced. For this, Sylvie is grateful. The dogs are gone, too, and though she doesn't ask about them, for a long time she will expect their sharp energetic barks, the frantic swinging of their tails as she moves about the yard.

THE WAR ENDS MANY TIMES

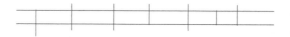

THE TRAIN ROCKS AS it climbs. Simone braces herself, but even
so the jostling nauseates her. Above, the bags slam against
each other in the metal racks. She has given up on sleep, though
tired, and stares out the window at the scraggly lilacs near the
tracks or farther out at the farms, the fields tinged with green,
the squat farmhouses like the one she grew up in. Near Dijon,
the train screeches to halt. The passengers in her car begin to
speak all at once. The women, surely sisters, in gray overcoats,
their gray hair pulled back in similar twists, are the loudest:
"What can it be? We'll be late for sure!" The elderly couple
that got on in the middle of the night looks at each other,
grimaces. The other passenger, a student in chemistry, judging
from his books, says to all of them and no one in particular,
"Damn!" His breath is stale and it hovers in the cabin for a
moment after he speaks, filling Simone with pity and dread.
The loudspeaker clicks on, buzzes, then goes silent. After a
pause, the conductor's voice comes on. "Attention, please,
Mesdames, Mesdemoiselles, and *Messieurs*, the bridge is out of service.
Everyone must get out, and cross the river on the pedestrian
bridge. Another train will take you the remaining distance to
Dijon." In the cabin, the passengers mutter and begin pulling

on coats. "Take all suitcases and parcels with you. This train is returning to Lyon."

Simone has placed her bags under her seat rather than struggle to lift them to the rack above. She is glad for this now, as she slides the valises from beneath her. *Concentrate*, she tells herself. She checks the clasps to see that they are tightly fastened and follows the chemistry student out of the cabin. The aisles are filled with passengers all pushing onwards, focused only on resuming their travels as soon as possible. Something—a coin? A marble?—drops, and Simone hears it ping against the floor. A child cries, and she thinks of her son Claude. It's been three months since she's seen him. She must get across this bridge, make her delivery, get to her son. She sees him as she left him last—on her mother's hip, his dark eyes drooping with fatigue. The suitcases feel heavy and cumbersome already.

Outside the air is moist. It will rain today, she thinks, perhaps even before she is across the bridge. Because the pedestrian bridge is narrow, there is some pushing and grumbling. Simone would rather wait until the bulk of the passengers move on, but it is difficult to slow in the crowd. She is pushed along with the others, the suitcases banging against her shins. Halfway across, the crowd thins and she can see over the river to where the train's narrow bridge ought to be. Her arms ache, so she sets the bags down for a minute and looks. The bridge dangles like a pendant on one side. The other side is simply gone, as is the trestle and part of the hillside. There is a gash in the dark earth where it was. Bombed, she understands, and she wonders by whom.

"Mademoiselle, you find this amusing?"

Beside her is a German officer, tall and unrumpled by travel.

She is aware then of a faint smile on her face—not a grin. Surely, she has not become so hardened to violence, such an admirer of destruction? The German is about her age, twenty-five or so, and unremarkable except for his eyes. Pale green, they assess Simone, take in her slim height, her blondeness, but give nothing back.

"It doesn't look real, does it?"

"But it is real, and a terrible nuisance for those who wish to go from one place to another."

"Yes, of course," Simone agrees. "Terrible." Her heart is beating too fast. She can hear it pounding in her ears. It seems impossible that the officer doesn't hear it as well. "It made me think of my son and his train set. "

"Are you on your way to your boy, then? To your family?"

"No, I'm on my way to visit a friend who is ill." There has been no reason to lie—she is to see Claude after the drop—so why has she?

"Both pretty and thoughtful," the officer says, looking her straight in the eye, unsmiling.

"*Merci*," Simone says. She smiles and bends to pick up her bags.

"Allow me," the officer says.

"I'm fine, really," Simone says. "You are too kind."

"You must save your strength for nursing your friend," he says, "and for your little boy." He shakes his index finger at her as if she is a child herself.

"It's you that is the thoughtful one," Simone says, "but I must warn you, the bags are heavy."

The last passengers have passed them now. In the distance, Simone can hear the train she is to board. She has received training. She has been taught how to behave if she suspects danger. If the bags are inspected—if it gets to that—she is to act shocked by the contents beneath the false bottom. She should insist that she is carrying them for a friend. She imagines the fright will turn her white-faced. She could faint, if need be. But she understands this will not be necessary. The German officer has made up his mind about her in that way that people do, men do.

"Good God," he says lifting them, "what do you have in here?"

"Nothing much" Simone says, "just some pistols."

"And a sense of humor, too," he says, laughing.

"Please, this will go to my head," Simone says. Her laughter is raspy and shrill in her ears.

At the train, the officer installs her in first class, though her ticket is for second only. "I will speak to the conductor," he says. He slides her suitcases under her seat.

The other passengers don't meet her eyes. She wants to protest, but of course, she cannot. What would she say? She is still shaking when the train departs in the rain. She sleeps hard until Dijon, wakes with a start like Claude used to when he'd cried himself to sleep. She is relieved to see her contact, whom she knows only as Monsieur Bruno, to pass on the suitcases she has brought from Lyon. It is easier when she carries documents, papers that will allow escape or an altered identity. When it is hardware, she usually adopts a kind of vagueness about what she carries, thinking only in terms of needs and supplies, a luxury, this line of thought, she sees now. Even though they are out of her possession, she sees the guns clearly, their grease and heft, the steely glint of them as she drinks a coffee in the train-station café.

SHE CAN'T REMEMBER A time she was so glad to see her mother's house, its shuttered windows like worried eyes. Inside, she breathes in the familiar smells of cooking and mothballs, her mother's rose perfume, the faintest trace of the tobacco that was her father's end.

"Claude," she says when she sees him on the kitchen floor with his toy tractor. Nearly three years old, he is making engine sounds with his lips. He stops the movement, but his lips still hum. He looks up at Simone.

"Grandmère," he calls, "come here."

Simone starts to crouch near him, but he darts away to her mother. Simone has moved too fast, swooped down too suddenly. She feels like a big clumsy bird, her hands, greedy talons. She should've let Claude come to her. She's gangly and awkward for the rest of the visit, knocking over a delicate vase, banging her head on the sloped ceiling in her old bedroom.

"Careful!" her mother says. "Watch yourself." She is, no doubt, thinking that if Simone had listened better to this advice long ago, she'd not be in the situation she is in—unwed, the mother of a child who fears her, a disgrace to the memory of her father.

She no longer fits here. When did this happen? Perhaps it was even before her time at the university and her brief affair with Claude's father, a classmate from the advanced mathematics seminar. But certainly it is true now, she thinks watching her mother cook beneath the blue-eyed gaze of Pétain. Simone knows enough to say nothing to her mother of her work or politics.

BACK IN LYON, SHE is distracted all the next day, unable to focus on her tasks at the accountant's office where she works. The numbers and columns seem to move beneath her eyes; she cannot keep the sums in her mind. "Perhaps you are unwell," Monsieur Fallard says, noting her shaky hands above the smudged columns.

"Just tired," she says, erasing again her errors.

That evening when she goes to the apartment on rue Chapelle to see if there is a delivery for her, she is easily persuaded to join the party that has begun. It's Martine's birthday, and several bottles of wine have been scrounged. A girl Simone hasn't seen before is playing the piano. After a couple of glasses, Simone finds herself telling Alain about the train, the bombed bridge, the officer. She thinks perhaps he will want to send her for more training or limit her territory. Simone expects to be reprimanded, but instead Alain laughs, a low rumbling laugh. This is the only appropriate response. What else can be said? She is laughing, too, when Alain takes her hand and pulls her from the settee and out onto a small balcony. From here she can see a small park, empty at this hour. The night air is balmy, and this makes the space feel intimate like a bath or the laundry, some place of steam and water, dirt falling away. She is a bit drunk, she realizes, her hand still in Alain's.

"Smart girl, " Alain says.

Words, all words, seem suspect, not something one can trust. "Shh," she says. What does she believe in? This man. This moment. He isn't much taller than her and so their bodies fit together easily, and she has that feeling one has after searching for a puzzle piece and then finding it—the certainty of the fit. Yes, this is the one. She believes in this.

THEY ARE TOGETHER EVERY night from now on, unless one of them is traveling. And when they've been apart, their lovemaking is particularly intense. She thinks of storms, of thunder, its big clamor. Sometimes she awakens to find they are moving together. In the lemony light of morning or the pitch of deep night, she responds immediately, has responded, it seems, before waking. With Alain, in these moments, she feels not so much safe as free from the awareness of danger, the need for safety. Waking, her limbs still buzzing from their exertions, she is shocked by her forgetting, her greed in this comfort.

Alain tells her about his daughter, Eugénie, who is six and living with his sister and her husband. In the photo he shows

Simone, the little girl has a high forehead like his. Freckles are sprinkled over her nose and full cheeks. And though she is smiling, Simone sees a watchfulness in her dark eyes. "*Mignonne*," she says. And when they see little girls with their parents in the streets, she asks, "Is Eugénie as tall as that one? Is she ready for a scooter, like that one has?" She knows little about the girl's mother, except that she died early in the war. "I was stationed at the Line and could not get away," he says. He shakes his head.

By this point in the war, such things—separations, deaths— are not uncommon. Not that one gets accustomed to them; no, one simply learns to train their thoughts elsewhere. Simone finds, however, that she cannot avoid thinking of his wife. She imagines her thrashing, feverish, angry at her husband for being away, though in her right mind she would know about duty and responsibility. Sick, however, she doesn't give a fig for such lofty notions.

In bed sometimes, they speak of how they will live after the war, how Alain will adopt Claude and the children will grow up siblings. There will be other children, too, and a big house with good sunlight, a garden in the back. He will return to medicine after the war. Simone will raise their children and help run his practice. It is so ordinary that Simone is surprised by her longing for it.

In late March, when she returns from a delivery to Marseille, there is a new courier, Brigitte. She is petite, dark haired, the friend of a friend from Metz. Her voice is high, flirty even when she is only asking about directions.

"He's your man?" she says, gesturing at Alain.

Simone dislikes the phrase—as she knows Alain would. They do not possess each other. What they have is both bigger and more encompassing. She doesn't want to explain all this to Brigitte. "Yes," she says.

"Handsome," Brigitte says, raising her eyebrows.

Brigitte talks only of boys, as if no other topic is worth discussion. She reports the boys she's encountered on her way to the apartment, how they looked at her and what this indicated. Did they like her? Were they going to ask her out? She made elaborate plans to run into them later. The next day it might be a different fellow, but always the planning and reporting, the giggles and strategy. And Alain notices her, too, though Simone doesn't blame him. Brigitte is impossible to ignore, leaning into everyone when she speaks, hip cocked, arms waving about.

"I'm not sure about Brigitte," she says to Alain.

"She's good at her work," Alain says.

And this is true; she's small enough to pass as a child. So Simone says nothing more, tucks away her concern. Is that what it is or is it petty jealousy? How can she know? And then, of course, there are other things to contend with. Alain's sister and husband and the girl are denounced in the Vaucluse, so they move to Le Puy. Alain has found them a place to live and work for Jean. The girl will start school there. There will be, perhaps, a chance to meet. And then, as if she understood that Simone and the others are weary of her chatter, Brigitte becomes quieter. She is less talkative, less excitable. Simone has to admit that she has settled down. Simone herself forgets her until she shows up with a bottle of wine or some cheese, procured, she says, through her landlord.

WHAT GOOD FORTUNE TO be in Paris at the same time, Simone thinks. She waits for Alain at a café, savoring her coffee. Late April is still cool, but she takes a table outdoors under an awning where the café is less crowded. It goes without saying that she doesn't know what Alain's business here is. Her own delivery—a bundle of papers from the Rhône area—went smoothly. The sky is as blue as a baby's bonnet. The rain-cleansed streets glitter now in the morning sun; the flowers in the beds bloom red and yellow. The Germans cannot prevent spring, she thinks. She watches Alain approach, his long strides. He's lost weight—they all have on war rations—and he looks wiry, like an athlete in training.

"Come," he says. "Let's walk."

"What is it?" Simone asks. They pass an elderly couple feeding pigeons from a park bench. The birds dart and waddle for the crumbs.

"Renaud has been arrested," Alain says.

Whatever calm and contentedness she has felt flaps off—a stupid, greedy pigeon into the bright blue sky.

"There's a leak somewhere," Alain says. "I can't say where—"

They've talked before about the Germans' desperation now that their loss is likely. The way it will be worse until it is better. Renaud is Alain's counterpart, the director of propaganda. It's too close.

Who suggests it first? Later Simone will try to recall, but it always seems as if they decided without speech, without deliberation. It is time to leave Lyon and their work. They see a sign in a building in the 14th arrondissement and the concierge lets them in. It's a bright spacious apartment, more extravagant than they are comfortable with. There are doors leading to a balcony overlooking a park.

"Charming," Alain tells the concierge. "But we've only started looking."

There are more signs and more apartments. One with a room perfect for a nursery, painted already a cheery yellow. Another has an excellent view of the Métro. It makes a racket when it passes, but Simone imagines Claude's delight watching the trains. Another still has dark busy wallpaper everywhere, even on the doors. It will have to come down, she thinks, all of it, but it doesn't seem difficult to manage. Her mind happily leaps forward. She'll need buckets and a scraper. Then, of course, for the move, boxes, a truck.

"After this is all over, we will have the most comfortable apartment in Paris," Alain says.

"But our work is over—or nearly," she says. "You have said so yourself."

Alain is silent beside her. "But this is the only way," she says.

"There is Eugénie to think of."

Alain's face tightens.

This tact is unfair, she understands. What she really means is *me, what about me?*

"I can't leave the others unguided," he says. "My place is with them."

"Of course," she says. "I understand." Simone is aware then of her feet throbbing, her fatigue. "I'll miss my train," she says, turning without a proper farewell. The tulips she passes on her way to Gare du Nord, the trees bursting into leaf are a reproach.

She does understand, but she is furious, nonetheless. She allows herself the train ride to stew—she loves him more than he loves her, he has chosen the cause over her, but why should this surprise her? This is part of what she has loved about him from the start. And yet, she knows that she is right; this is the only way they might both survive the stepped-up arrests and reprisals. Her anger started out pure and fierce, but by Lyon, she understands that it is also a distraction from what else she might feel.

EVEN WHEN ONE IS alert to danger, bad news comes as a shock. Then, of course, the bad news is never quite the bad news one expects: one afternoon, there is a telegraph from Besançon. Her mother has died in the night. Simone must come collect

Claude at once. Monsieur Fallard is kind when she tells him her news. "Go immediately," he says. "We will manage without you." Simone would like to tell Alain, but he is traveling. At the apartment, she looks for him. Only Brigitte is there, a pencil tucked behind her ear, a notebook on the table. "It's just me here," she says. "Martine just left."

Simone cannot hide her disappointment.

"*Biscuit?*" Brigitte says, tipping a box of cookies towards Simone.

They are Claude's favorite kind—a layer of chocolate pressed on top a sugary wafer. He likes to lick off the chocolate until the cookie collapses into mushy crumbs. And then Simone is telling her about her mother, about the need to fetch Claude.

"How old?"

"Just three," Simone says.

"I love children," Brigitte says. "I want plenty one day." Her hand flutters near her stomach and she seems on the verge of saying more, but stops. "Take these," she says, "for the boy." She folds up the package and hands it to Simone.

"Thank you," Simone says. She hadn't thought to bring anything for Claude, but, of course, he will need distraction and cajoling. She's unequipped. "Perhaps, I should wait until tomorrow," she says.

"No, no, no," Brigitte is adamant. "Your boy needs you."

The train station is crowded. There are German soldiers, naturally, but also groups of young people, students perhaps, their faces flushed and happy. It must be some summer program. Simone is able to get the last train for Besançon, though she has to run to board it. Perhaps if the train station were not so crowded, she would have seen Alain descending the northbound train, his brow creased in thought, in his pocket, a note from Eugénie who will turn seven later that month. *Dear Papa, For my birthday, I would like a doll with hair like mine* (brune). *Love, Eugénie.*

On the train, Simone takes a seat in an empty row. She closes her eyes, tries to calm her racing heart. In her hurry, she has brought nothing to read, nothing to eat except for the cookies for Claude. Eating one, it dawns on her: Brigitte is pregnant. It explains the fullness of her face, her concern for Claude. Soon, we'll be hearing about a wedding, Simone thinks, slipping into sleep. Who is the groom?

She isn't sure how long she has slept when she is awakened by the shuffling and movement of the other passengers. A German soldier is pacing the aisle, demanding identification. A child squawks several rows back, and the soldier seems to take this personally. As he turns, Simone sees that it's the same soldier who carried her bags across the river in March. When he comes to her seat, he recognizes her. "I see you are traveling lighter this time, *Fraulein*."

"Yes, light as a bird," she says, flapping her hands by her shoulders like wings.

The officer doesn't smile. Perhaps he thinks she's gone stupid. Maybe she's lost her appeal. It's true she hasn't run a brush through her hair all day. More likely he's worried about the Allies' progress toward Paris, but his disregard is unnerving. The doors stick open after he leaves her compartment, and she hears his voice all the way to the end of the car.

AT HER SISTER'S, SHE finds Claude subdued but in good health. His things are packed, her sister tells her pointedly, as if Simone might change her mind. Simone only thanks her. "You are so thoughtful," she says. "I must hurry back, a busy time, you can be sure." She keeps up the chatter, so there is no room for Natalie's questions or snipes.

Then they are back in Lyon. Since it is on the way to her apartment, she takes Claude to the park straight from the train station and promises him his own sailboat for the pond as soon as she can find one. "Would you like that, my little man?" The day has turned warm and sunny. Claude nods, takes her hand solemnly as he watches the other children play, their bright boats bobbing, and she feels something akin to hopefulness, perhaps it is hopefulness, though she can hardly recognize the feeling—gleaming and expansive, something bold about it. It seems possible in this moment that the parts of her life might be knit together into some satisfying future.

In her apartment, she shows Claude the settee where he will sleep. "We'll put sheets and blankets on it," she tells him.

"*D'accord*, Maman," he says, looking around at the stark room. Simone wishes she had made some effort with the apartment. She has hung nothing on the walls or windows, and compared to her mother's or her sister's house, hers doesn't look like a proper home. Temporary and provisional. "We'll go to Maman's office, but first we'll stop by some friends' place."

As they walk, Claude is singing a song she doesn't know. It makes no sense, as far as she can tell, but it is difficult to hear over the street noise. Surely the singing is a good sign, she tells herself. At the apartment, she is surprised to find the door ajar. "Hello," she calls, pushing the door in. Inside, more surprises: the table and chairs are overturned, the cupboard doors open. Papers are strewn. The piano bench is shattered by the back door. She must fight the impulse to right the furniture, tidy up this horrible mess. It is only a shard of glass dropping from the shattered window that pushes her from her the doorway, and this only because Claude has begun to cry from the crash.

From down the hallway, the door to the doctor's office opens, and a nurse calls down. "You mustn't linger. It's under surveillance still. *Allez!*"

But where will she go? How will she find out what has happened to Alain and the others? Where are they? What were the plans for such a situation, she cannot remember. On the

55

street holding Claude's hand, she walks without direction. The pedestrians—the old men in their caps, the nurses pushing prams, the secretaries who have taken off their cardigans on this, the first hot day—look sinister, suspicious, any one of them capable of treachery. Claude's tears have subsided to an occasional sniffle now. To look at him would make her cry, too, so she keeps her eyes trained on the street. She focuses on each step until they are again at her apartment. She cannot even think beyond opening her apartment door, getting Claude a drink of water, slipping off her shoes.

A WEEK PASSES WITHOUT a word from Alain. Simone knows, of course she does, but she doesn't permit herself to know. Considerable effort is required to keep out the horrible darkness edging into her consciousness. She tells herself how good Alain is with people—drawing them to his side, making them like him without even trying. Not even the SS can be impervious to his goodness. Sometimes, she must take another approach: the Germans will see that they're done for and retreat. Still other times she imagines an escape, so that when she hears footsteps in the hallway late at night, she is certain it is Alain. She throws open the door only to see the retreating back of her neighbor, home late from the café.

She writes to his sister at the address Alain left with her.

Dear Lise,

You will be wondering, I am sure, about your brother. I wish I wrote with better news. He has been detained. I saw him last on 29 July. He was in good spirits then.

What more can she say? She cannot write about the overturned desk at the apartment, the shattered window. There is nothing in which to nestle the news of the arrest—no details, no pleasantries about the weather or even words of familiarity.

Even her slanted scrawl on the page seems blunt to her, horrible. How unfortunate that none of them believe in God because prayer might be useful, something she could mention here. Instead she concludes: *You three are very much in my thoughts.*

She seals the envelope and posts it the next morning, her hands shaking as she passes over the envelope.

AT NIGHT, WHEN CLAUDE sleeps, she writes other letters, letters that she cannot send. *My darling, Alain,* they all begin. In these letters she might jump from the past to the future in a single sentence. She might remind him of Paris, how they might have gotten away. Sometimes she cajoles as if this is still possible, the only difficulties involving leases, boxes, a truck. Sometimes she writes about Eugénie and Claude holding hands, about the baby she and Alain will have that will bind their families into one. She describes the photograph they will have taken—she knows the very studio on rue des Fleurs—of the baby cradled between the older children. She writes, shocking herself, about her desire, how she misses their bodies in a tumble, the urgency and the collapse. And then, remembering Alain's cautiousness about papers—phone numbers scrawled on napkins, addresses, receipts, names or dates—she burns them.

Of course, one second-guesses, grasps at the many missed opportunities for escape—that lovely word, that flowing cape of an idea! Why did they not attach themselves to it when it flapped and hovered close? Why?

AND THEN THE AMERICANS are in the streets, in their tanks and trucks, their faces shiny with victory. Everyone is singing and kissing and passing open bottles of champagne. And Simone, too, is drawn into the celebration. She drinks from the bottle passed her way. She lifts Claude onto her shoulders so he can wave at the soldiers. He is passed a small American flag, and he flaps it about. There are other treats that day as well—chewing gum and chocolate. Simone's pockets are stuffed with his bounty. By the end of the day, her feet are bricks. They've walked from *centre-ville* to the outskirts of the city and back. She sleeps as if drugged, despite the celebrating that goes on in the streets until early morning.

Later that week, there is a knock at her door: Martine, looking pale, is before her, circles the color of bruises beneath her eyes. Simone's heart leaps to her throat so she is unable to speak. "Where?" she manages. "Where is he?"

"The men are gone," Martine says.

Simone hears her, but the individual words are hollow, unrecognizable. Neither can she string the words together; just as she gathers them, one darts off, a bead from a broken necklace. She hears it clacking across the wood floor. But no, that is Martine's heels. She is moving to embrace Simone who is making another sort of noise—low and ragged, animal.

"I'm sorry," Martine says, holding her. She leads her to the settee, makes her sit while she rummages in the cupboard. She finds an old bottle of brandy and pours them each a large glass.

"Tell me," Simone says. The brandy tastes burnt. She believes she must have the details to absorb this news.

Martine drinks her brandy quickly. She pours another and then tells Simone about the arrest. The Germans came to the apartment that evening just as everyone had returned from their various errands. They handcuffed men and women together. Threw them into cells at Montluc prison and then left them. Later, hungry and filthy, they were interrogated. Beaten—the men particularly. And then when the Germans saw the writing on the wall, they took the men out to the country and shot them against an abandoned house and then set it on fire. They planned to do the same for the women but ran out of time.

"We were left in our cell," Martine says. "And do you know those animals were drinking champagne while they packed up?"

It was Brigitte, Martine says, who'd turned them in. She'd been sleeping with a Kraut.

Of course, Simone thinks. She'd known Brigitte with her boy craziness and her wiggly need for attention couldn't be trusted, but she'd ignored this. Why? Because it looked like something else—jealousy, pettiness, and who can say even now that it wasn't those as well? And then she was distracted by her own affairs. By Alain. She thinks of Brigitte folding up the package of cookies for Claude, telling her to go. *Your boy needs you.*

Simone is crying again and Martine brings her tissues. Then Claude is before her in his woolen pajamas, his face flushed with sleep.

"Maman? he says. "Why are you crying?"

"Go back to bed," Simone says, but she pulls him tight, breathes in his little boy smell. She feels his shoulder blades, his fragile bones.

After Martine leaves, Simone goes to the hiding place. Alain has kept a box beneath the floorboards in her hallway. It is a small cardboard box, coated on top with a layer of dust and cobwebs. She wipes the lid carefully and then removes it. Inside there are photographs. Here is one of Alain holding the girl aloft and grinning at her. They are in front of a small stucco house, the kind common on the Normandy coast. In another photo, the girl is seated in a *poussette*, her whole hand stuffed into her mouth. Her legs are as plump as sausages. There is a photo of Alain and his wife. She is tiny next to him, her nose and chin sharp. They squint into the camera. Behind them there is only sky, as if they are complete. They need no one, though of course there is the photographer. There are no photographs like this of Simone and Alain, and this lack makes her cry again.

There are letters from Lise, too, with her reports of the girls' days—her growth, her good marks in school. She has nearly completed a sampler of the alphabet. She is moved up at the end of term. She is strong willed and refuses to apologize to Jean for some infraction involving a card game. Simone reads this old news carefully, seeking what, she isn't sure. She holds the pages to her nose, but none of Alain' smell—pine and cigarettes, salt—remains. There is one chiding remark—that of a married sister to her brother—about his fling. The word rankles. How can this not feel like another loss? She has lost Alain and any claim to him. The wedding ring slides at he bottom of the box. It's a simple silver band—not expensive. Simone slips it on her right hand. It fits and like that, she decides it is hers. With her thumb, she rolls it around on her finger. This is pleasant, soothing, perhaps in the way the rosary was for her mother, something to touch and hold, when so much else slips through our hands.

She writes Lise telling her of her sorrow. She tries to explain how close she and Alain were, how fast love grew up between them. If you were drawn a warm bath at the end of a cold rainy day, would you dip in only your toes? If you were given a bar of chocolate, would you eat just one square? Pleasure will not be parceled out, not when so much is uncertain. But she cannot tell his twin sister that. She describes their plans—their marriage, the children. The way they wavered between moving to America and staying in France, which would need their care after the war. Do these plans become more elaborate, more certain as she writes? She no longer knows herself.

> *He was magnificent, Alain, as you know.*
> *Each night I feel so alone, so terribly alone after all the awfulness.*

I have your last letters to Alain, Lise. I know how close you were. He hid only his sentiments for me. No, Lise, what we had was not some flirtation, not by a long shot. I can assure you our happiness was perfect this past summer. We never wanted to be apart for even a second, because as Alain would say, our time could at any moment be cut short. It was. But at least I have those moments.

In the end she sends nothing. And then one day there is a letter from Jean. They are coming through Lyon and want to visit with her. There is little time to prepare. And still not much to buy in the market, but she does procure some potatoes, a little cheese.

SIMONE HAS IMAGINED THAT Lise would look like Alain—all sharp angles—but Lise is softer, rounder, her coloring lighter. They don't even look like siblings, let alone twins. Lise's red hair is pulled up into a thick twist. Her eyes are golden-brown. And her walk is crooked, she leans into Jean as she moves. Yet for all her softness, Simone finds she cannot tell her all she had planned. It seems foolish to insist on the love of a man who is gone. Besides, Lise has her own stories to tell. "Do you know," Lise says, "I begged him not to return. He knew—we both knew—what he was returning to. If only I'd insisted." She shakes her head. *If only.*

The girl—what can she say of this child who was nearly hers? Alain is everywhere in her—the high rounded forehead, the quick laugh. Simone finds that she cannot look at her for very long. She has bought her a doll with golden hair in braids and a blue-checked dress. It is both too much and too little, she understands, presenting it. As they are leaving, Simone remembers the box of letters and photos. "Wait," she says, and she returns with the box, hands it to Lise.

THE WAR ENDS NOT once, in a single moment, but many times for Simone—and perhaps it is this way for others, too. First, the Germans departing, the Americans in the street, the flags waving, Martine's report. Then one day there is meat in the markets, tarts again in the windows of the *pâtisserie*. Simone buys an autumn frock. Later, there is a letter from Lise and Jean detailing their plans; they are moving to America. Then, from California, they will write about the weather, the frustrating idiosyncrasies of English, a trip to Mt. Rushmore, but nothing about Alain or the past. That time is over, they seem to say, a lid on a box snapped shut. It is with this view that Simone marries, in the new year, a widower, with a daughter two years older than Claude. Her husband is a large man, broad-shouldered and sturdy, with a head of thick white hair. "My pet," he calls her and doesn't like for her to be far from his side.

Later and for many years, when she is waiting for a streetlight to change or in line for a teller at the bank—always moments when she is forced to slow—her thoughts will travel back to that time, to Alain, to how things might have turned out. In particular, she imagines that she saw him at Gare du Nord the evening she left to fetch Claude and Alain was returning from Le Puy. Through the crowd, they see each other at the same moment, surprise giving way to delight and relief—it's like looking in the mirror. Alain pulls her to him. He smells of travel, of sweat and smoke, but she breathes him in. Over the singing and games of the schoolchildren, she explains her mother's death, the need to fetch Claude. And this is her favorite part: "I'll come with you," Alain says, lifting his valise.

This is the only way that the outcome might have been otherwise, not without its own complications and lasting aches, she knows. She is not so naïve as to think that. Simone follows him onto the train, into a car where they find seats together. He will purchase his ticket on board. In this whole time, they have never traveled together, and now here they are. This will be the first of many trips, they decide. Where else will they go? Athènes, Copenhague, Mongolie, Pérou, Mexique. "St. Petersburg, Florence," Alain might say. "Québec, Chicago, Rio, where we will dance in the streets." Their list is long and indiscriminate, the possibilities endless.

GENERATIONS

HENRI DUVAL SQUATS BY a beanpole and yanks a weed. He stands, rubs his lower back, surveys the rest of the garden. It is doing especially well this year. Each spring he plants it as his father planted it and his grandfather before him. Why change what has worked? As a younger man, he was sometimes tempted by a potato promised to be blight-free, or a reseeding lettuce but they were never, in fact, superior. He has learned his lesson. At the tomato row, he stops to pick. The plum tomatoes aren't yet ripe, but the Picardies, warm from the sun, drop into his palm like floozies. He is gathering the last when he hears the cars. The road is far enough away that he cannot make out faces in the black Citroëns, just the shape of their caps and shoulders. Three cars. A black smear through the green fields. What are they up to now? By this point in the war, he has had more than enough of the Boches. In the city, he has heard, they are behaving worse than ever. They are like cornered animals, hissing and clawing rather than running off while they might. A schoolteacher was shot in front of her students last week.

He will say nothing of the Boches to Berthe when he goes in for dinner. He is in the habit of telling her little because all topics lead to her favorite: the need to move to Lyon to be near their daughter. Thérèse is expecting, and this has added fodder to Berthe's grand scheme.

His resolve makes no difference. He has no sooner set the basket of vegetables by the sink than she starts in on him.

"Who keeps a grandmother from her grandchild? A new mother from her own mother at a time like this?"

"Berthe, let us eat in peace."

"Are you made of stone?" The pea soup sloshes in his bowl when she sets it before him, but it smells tasty.

"What beautiful soup," he says. He takes a spoonful. "I might like a bit of salt, however."

She thrusts the small bowl at him.

He could remind her of the way she barely tolerated his mother when Thérèse, then Jacqueline, were born. Oh, she had seethed at the advice and directives! She will deny this, he knows, and it is true that the two grew to love each other. It was Berthe, in the end, who nursed his mother, spoonfed her soups and pureed fruit as if she were her child. He misses his mother still, his father, too. And his grandparents, all of them gone now. He misses the way they all gathered at the end of the day—tired and sweaty but with a solid day's work behind them, the aches and sore muscles proof of essential tasks undertaken. The land is all he has left of them, of that time. In his memories, it is always a day like this one: golden and blue, the sweetness of cut hay in the air. Of course, this cannot be true. It rains often and the wind whips up, especially in the fall. His grandfather was known, from time to time, to drink too much. The women bickered over the proper way to roast a bird, but that is a faint murmur alongside his version. If this makes him sentimental, foolish, *tant pis.*

"You're an old man. When will you see?"

"I see, I see," he says. "The work is good for me."

"Who would know to help us if we took ill? If something happened? They would find our bodies, rotting, is that what you want?"

He slurps the last of his soup and begins on the chicken. "Delicious," he says and this is his answer to her question. His train of thought is this: good chicken from his own coop, fed with grain from his fields, fields that were his father's and his grandfather's and so on for generations. He isn't going anywhere.

"I'll go without you, Henri."

"I would miss your soup."

"You're a goat," Berthe says. "A stubborn old goat."

As a peace offering of sorts, he tells her of the convoy of Boches earlier. "Three cars of them," he says. "What are they doing out here now?"

"They have hearty appetites," she says.

"But why then did they not stop here? Not that I want them, mind you."

She snorts. "They do what they want."

On this they agree.

"Go on, then," she says. "Have your rest, old man."

Something in her expression—a wistfulness and determination both—reminds him of the girl he married. The prettiest girl in Saint-Genis-Laval, with a laugh like a bell, golden hair in plaits down her back. The years have given her bulk. She is squat and square, her movements stiff. Her hair is gray and wrapped into a fat bun at the back of her head. Still, it seems to him that he did the only thing he could have—stepped forward as if offered a glass of cold water straight from the well, gulped it down.

That she now thinks only of the future—the grandchild that is to be born, the ones to come after that—is not surprising, really. Perhaps all marriages are divided like this, one person tending to the future, the other to the past in the way that other tasks are divided—the kitchen and the barn, for instance. The bedroom has stayed cool, despite the day's warmth. It is shaded by an old oak, and as he dozes off, he hears the leaves rustling in the breeze.

When he awakes, he hears gunshots. The noise seems to be coming from the old fort. Target practice, he thinks. It is late in the game for that. But he has given up trying to understand the Germans.

In the kitchen Berthe is making jam with the last of the raspberries. The smell of fruit is heavy in the steamy air. Here, all he hears is her clanging and banging about, the big kettle boiling away on the stove. Berthe ladles the hot liquid into the jars. When she turns back, he swipes a spoonful, blows on it, and then smears in on a piece of bread left from lunch.

"I'm going to the back orchard," he tells her back.

Outside, though, he turns the other way, toward the hilly wooded area near the fort. He knows they are up to no good. Of course, he knows this. But he must see in the same way he would check on the livestock during a heavy rain. This vigilance comes with the territory; it is something he has inherited like his father's lumpy nose and square jaw. He startles as the shots start up again, cracking through the quiet.

Near the edge of his property, he stumbles over a tree root. It's not a bad fall, he thinks, though he's torn his trousers. Berthe will patch them, won't even question him about the cause of the tear. They are old pants, patched already. But when he tries to stand, a pain shoots up his left leg. His ankle throbs. Near the path, he spots a long stick. This is no time to turn infirm, feeble. He can hear Berthe calling him an old man and this propels him forward. Yes, this stick will do nicely, he thinks.

Once he develops a rhythm, the pain seems to lessen. Surprising what we can get accustomed to, he thinks. He takes small steps, treats the left leg gingerly. He is sweating when he makes it to the top of the hill. He takes his handkerchief from his pocket and wipes his brow. It is hot even in the shade.

He sets his stick by the side of the pine, where he can reach it easily on his way down. Near the base of the tree, the branches are close together. An easy climb, though his hands quickly get sticky with sap. In addition to the shots coming from the fort, he hears shouting, too.

When he can see to the fort clearly, he stops climbing. He observes the Citroëns parked at the foot of the long drive. There are buses, their windows painted over, parked near the crumbling fort wall. There is writing on the buses, but he cannot make out the words, though he understands from the barred windows that they are from Montluc prison. Men and women are herded from the bus and marched in groups to the caretaker's cottage. They are tied together in twos, and they stumble going the short distance. This provokes more shouting—in French—from the civilians who are doing the Germans' bidding. When the prisoners are lined up in a way that pleases the officers, the shooting commences. Before he understands what he is watching, the bodies crumple and fall. Quickly blood pools in the dust. The officer gives a word then, and the civilians begin dragging the bodies into the cottage. Like bags of grain, he thinks, with less care even than that.

His heart is banging around in his chest. He should get down, go back, but he is pinned here, it seems.

How many times do they repeat this action? Five more? Ten? He tries to keep count. Something in his brain, some basic function has ceased working. Past the fort, he sees the stream where he liked to skip rocks as a boy, where his girls waded on days like this one. He can make out the red tiled roofs of town, the church steeple. What a nursery tale, that. God in Heaven. There is nothing.

The men circle the cottage, splashing it with petrol. Then, from the back window, there is a streak of movement. Two prisoners have escaped, then a third. They run toward the fields. Before Henri has a chance to root for them, the shots commence. Two of the prisoners fall, but the third keeps going, leaping over hedges at the perimeter of the fort. Two soldiers are dispatched after him. The prisoner disappears into the trees of the adjoining property. Henri knows that land. It is hilly, brambly. There are few places to hide.

The sun, so good for his crops, is good, too, for fire, and soon the cottage is engulfed in flames. From the cars, bottles of champagne are brought out and passed around. The men are fast drinkers. They make a game of tossing the empties.

He finds he is shaking, everything swimmy, blurred, as if he is the one drinking champagne in the heat of the day. Henri starts down the tree. He needs water to drink, solid ground, but his legs are not easily governed. Great concentration is required. With each step, the pain in his ankle flares dependably. This seems all he might count on. What a fool he has been to think there was anything else.

At the foot of the tree, he reaches for his stick. His legs work better on the ground, but the wooziness persists. He must lean into the ivy to vomit. And again. When he wipes his mouth with his shirtsleeve, he sees a streak of red. Blood? No, it's Berthe's raspberry jam. And then he is retching again, emptying himself, the whole of his gut.

When he reaches his house, its sameness is an affront. The wheelbarrow is where he left it, the soil and compost drying as he had intended. The geraniums are lushly red in their window boxes. There, on the front step, are his rain boots. The door swings open.

"You're hurt," Berthe says. She doesn't wait for his response but takes him by the arm. "Come, sit. I'll clean you up." She gets a cloth and moistens it at the sink, wipes his face and neck. "Let's get this shirt off."

Henri watches her unbuttoning his shirt. He smells his sweat on it, his vomit and the smoke from the cottage. The shirt is torn, he sees, and Berthe balls it up.

"Ruined," she says, but she is using the gentle voice she used with the girls when they were little and sick or hurt or just sad, the voice she will use with their grandbaby—and soon, because there is nothing to keep him here any longer. Ruined. He lets her voice wrap around him, a soft blanket of concern. She bends to unlace his boots. She must struggle to get the left one off. Each tug hurts. Then both boots are off and his feet are soaking in a tub of water. Cool water. His foot is swollen, purple and ugly.

"After this, you will lie down," Berthe says.

He nods.

As she leads him to their bedroom, he hears an explosion from the fort. Berthe turns and squints at him, questioning. But what can he say? He slips between the covers of the bed. The explosions continue until dark. When they stop, the quiet is no relief. It is nothing he can count on.

The Germans decamp within ten days. Henri cannot celebrate with his friends and neighbors because his ankle remains swollen, tender.

When he can walk easily, Henri will make his way to the municipal building to report what he's seen. Already, though, others have come forward. From his attic window, the police chief, Monsieur Hubert, observed the prisoners being led from the buses, though the fort wall obscured some of his view. Monsieur Bernard heard the shots as he worked in his field. The report indicates that between 110 and 120 political prisoners from the Montluc jail were killed that day.

71

Besides the bodies and the body parts, these items are found in the wreckage of the cottage: several wedding bands, a Bible, hernia trusses, a hair clip in the shape of a shell. And this: an infant's crib shoe. Someone's memento, the report concludes, because there were no children's bodies found inside.

By October, Henri and Berthe are installed in their new apartment on rue Saint Jacques. The farm is sold to a forward-thinking businessman from Metz. When he is born, Thérèse's baby, a boy she names Hugo after Henri's father, has a birth certificate free of German insignia or words. Everyone agrees this is a fine thing.

HUNGER

IT IS EASY ENOUGH to borrow a car, but petrol is another story.
The trains, on the other hand, are delayed by damaged tracks,
bombed bridges, and God knows what else. Sometimes the
trains don't appear. Or if they do show, you might find yourself
crowded into the aisle outside the compartment or without a
space at all. In the end, he hitches a ride to Rive-de-Gier and
from there, another ride to Lyon. From the highway, he walks
into town. It's hot for October, so he's sweating when he gets
to the prison, in need of a bath, a fresh shirt. His face and neck
are red and tight with sunburn. He considers stopping in a café
for a beer, a bite to eat, but he pushes on. He has come this far
fueled by rage; surely it can carry him the rest of the way. Since
they learned of Brigitte's part in Alain's arrest, Jean's thoughts
have been full of violence, of breaking her, shaking some sense
into her, his hands tight on her neck. He hasn't told anyone
this, certainly not Lise, who is herself broken with grief.

At the prison he learns this sad fact: there isn't room for all
those turned in for collaboration, so some prisoners are being
held in makeshift cells in a nearby office building. She is there,
he's told when he gives her real name. For so long they have
spoken of her as Brigitte, her code name, that he flubs her real

name and must repeat it for the guards. Jean is directed up the street.

At the building, he goes to the first floor office, where the reception is set up. Guards smoke in the small waiting room of what was once a doctor's office. Beneath the smoke, Jean can smell the medicinal tang of bandages and salves, rubbing alcohol. Papers and files are stacked on the examining table. A chart detailing the digestive tract remains on the far wall.

Again he tells the guards his business, again he stumbles over her name, but once he's said it right, the guard grunts. "She's here, all right," he says, rising. He takes a key ring off a hook and gestures for Jean to follow him. "Who is she to you?"

"She turned in my wife's brother."

"Then you won't mind me saying she's a stupid cow, that one."

Jean follows him down a narrow hallway.

"We've got the cellar divided into several cells." He opens a door to a flight of uneven wooden stairs. The air smells sharply of mildew, and the single bulb emits only a sour light. Down they go, the guard first. Thrust into the damp cold, Jean shivers.

At the foot of the stairs, they pass a door that is bolted shut. Through a small window, Jean sees only darkness. The guard stops and unlocks the next door. Jean expects to be let in alone, but the guard comes in with him. A small barred window near the ceiling provides the only light in the cell. In this light, dust particles drift, thickly. Jean's eyes take a moment to adjust. There is a pallet in the far corner and on it a body, too small, he thinks at first, to be a grown woman. And then he remembers that Alain had claimed her size was a benefit. She'd been hired because she could pass as a boy.

"Sit up," the guard says, "show some respect to your visitor."

The body turns and Jean sees the swollen belly beneath the blue prison gown. She's no boy now. She heaves herself upright, groaning. He sees her shaved head, the dark bristles where the hair is growing back and the bloody nicks from the razor.

The guard lifts a tray from the floor. The empty dishes rattle as he stands. Jean catches a whiff of cabbage. "She sure puts it away," the guard says. "Knock when you're done with her." The door clicks shut behind him with chilly finality. Jean shivers again. Why has he come here? Before he can begin to answer himself, she starts talking. It takes Jean a moment to understand what she's saying because her voice is faint, the speech of a child.

"I didn't know what would happen, that it would end the way it did . . . I never thought . . ."

"Are you a fool?" The newspaper article about her trial mentioned she was employed as a music teacher before her work for the Germans.

"I don't know," she says. She sounds as if she is considering this possibility.

He steps closer and she flinches.

The skin on her arms and legs is various shades of injury—plum, yellow-green, maroon. Her arm, he sees, is broken, and it hangs crookedly, like a damaged wing.

"Who are you? Did you tell me already?" she asks.

"Never mind who I am." He will give her nothing, not his name, not forgiveness. "I'll ask the questions here."

"I'm sorry," she says. "You can't imagine how sorry I am."

"Why did you turn them in?"

"I loved him," she says through a sob. "He said we'd marry after the war."

This is what she said in her trial, too. That she loved the German for whom she was working. As if one could not argue with love. As if that excused what it wrought.

"I would do anything for him. You know what that is like, don't you, to love someone like this?"

75

Jean believes he does, but he isn't giving her this. "My niece is an orphan thanks to you and your love."

"I told you I'm sorry," she says.

"That's not enough," he says, stepping toward her.

He has known women like this before, women who hunger above all else for a man. That he has perhaps benefitted from this attitude in the past is sickening. "Where is he now, your boyfriend?"

"I don't know," she says, and her sniffling commences again.

"Is that all you can say?" There is no pleasure in the breaking of a broken thing, only queasy shame. How could he have thought otherwise? Outside the barred window, black guard boots walk one way, then the other.

Alain is gone and this creature, still speaking of love and devotion, is alive. But what can he do to right this? Nothing, and this is not enough. He had thought before he arrived here that he wouldn't be able to contain his hatred, his anger, but in fact, it has slipped away from him, and now without a float, he's plunged under a giant wave.

"They forced themselves on me, the men who brought me here, all but one of them who wouldn't because of the baby."

He needs to get out of here, away from her. In Le Puy, Lise is probably making supper. He imagines Lise, her long hair pulled back, looking out the window into the courtyard, waiting for the girl to come in from her play. She had begged Alain not to go back to Lyon that last visit. She'd known it was coming—his arrest—in the way she often knew things about him, without words. Alain had known, too, but he'd said his comrades needed him.

"I had to eat," she says, introducing a new tone. She strokes her belly with her good arm.

"Shut up," he says, but without venom, as if swatting away a fly. He knows what she was paid for her work for the Germans because it was in the newspaper, the bonuses for good work. She no doubt feasted every night.

What will happen to this child, he wonders. Who will raise him, tell him the sad story of his conception? Brigitte has been condemned to death, though he suspects she'll be pardoned in the long run. Already in the papers there are rumblings of forgiving and forgetting, of moving on.

He pounds on the door to let the guard know he is done. He doesn't look back; he knows she is again curled up on her bed, a crumpled heap, whimpering.

His mouth is dry. He couldn't even spit if he were so inclined.

WHEN HE STUMBLES OUT of the building, he is blinded by the sunlight. He has expected to exit into darkness, but not that much time has passed, less than thirty minutes in total. The shops are still open, and business is brisk. Men smoke in the café across the street. On a bench, a child, younger than Eugénie, holds something blue and yellow—a flower? No, it's a toy, a pinwheel. In darkness he would have time to adjust his features, mask what he feels. This huge hopelessness. It must frighten people, his face, because they move away from him as he walks. A woman in a pink cloche narrows her eyes at him, pulls her parcel close as he passes.

He turns into a small park. He will sit for a moment, he thinks, then get a room, some dinner. He has told Lise only that he had some matters to take care of in Lyon, and not to expect him until morning. He is exhausted. Even his fingers ache. Beneath a statue of Rousseau, an old woman, a kerchief tied under her chin, is feeding the pigeons. The birds lunge and peck at the breadcrumbs. He is surprised by the immense hate he has for the greedy things, their awful flapping. He stomps through them, scattering them. The woman curses at him. "Bastard," she says, "what did they do to you?"

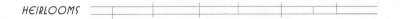

She isn't as old as he thought. She's got plenty of years left for feeding birds; generations of pigeons will grow fat from her efforts. Nothing is as it seems. Nothing. Already, the oily birds are waddling back, their hunger enormous, without end.

EN VOYAGE

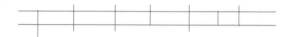

IT IS AN UNATTRACTIVE business, this, but it must be done. And he is the only one who can do it. Lacey's parents are dead and there are no other relations. On paper, he is her husband still. He corrects himself: her widower. And what he feels cleaning out the house where once he lived with her—quite happily for awhile—could be mistaken for a widower's grief. He cries and sweats, dampening both his handkerchiefs. He enters rooms and finds he has forgotten what he came for. He must retrace his steps to remember. Ah, yes—a box, a roll of tape, something into which he can separate all these items, the detritus of Lacey's life. Maybe grief isn't ever pure, he thinks, maybe it is always diluted by guilt—for things done or left undone, for infractions large and small. And there is the possibility, too, that guilt is easier than grief, in its familiarity, its sly shuffling of self to the forefront.

Lucien lifts a framed photograph from the dresser—it's of him in his tuxedo, Lacey in her stage getup and Tiny sitting with his front paws up. One of their early publicity photos. *The gams on that girl*, he thinks. Lacey, Lacey, Lacey. This has been her dramatic final exit. How disappointed she'd be to know that her death has received little notice. World events eclipsed the suicide of a former radio celebrity; there wasn't even a proper obituary, only the tiniest write-up in the *San Francisco Chronicle*. Lucien sets the photo into the box to discard. Where is the dog? He whistles. "Tiny?" he calls. "Where are you?"

In the backyard, the gate is open. Tiny's dish is overturned on the patio. God only knows, Lucien thinks, looking down the street, past the other stucco bungalows, the palm-lined parkway. Tiny is gone, like so much else. It's getting hot, and it's still only morning. He should move into the attic before it becomes unbearable. In the rest of the house he was faced with clutter—dishes in the sink, clothes piled on the bed and vanity stool, magazines and books left open on the floor as if they might be returned to at any moment. And this is the most disturbing: flowers rotting in a vase on the coffee table. Maroon and yellow iris, a flower he has always disliked with its petals like tongues, the shock of purple fur. And now he wonders how the same person can cut flowers, arrange them in a vase and then later—how much later?—swallow all her sleeping pills. Maybe this is the wrong question, he thinks, taking the attic stairs two at a time, but what is the right question?

When he opens the attic door, something scurries under the low rafters into the shadowy place where the roof joins the sides of the house. He opens an old wardrobe by the door. It's crammed full of dresses. The fabrics—stiff and shiny—rustle as he reaches in. The dresses have held onto Lacey's smell, a warm, spicy scent that has soured in the folds of the material. He stuffs the gowns into the garbage sack. Sweat collects on his forehead and under his collar. It is uncomfortable up here, but he won't complain. He never complains about the heat, and when others do, he laughs. "You can't be serious?" he says. "This is the life!" In Montpon, which he remembers as cold, always cold, his time was spent looking for ways to get warm, his hands and ears and feet.

To the bag of dresses he adds a pair of chintz drapes, a hatbox, and some quilts. He wants none of this for himself, and Beatrice wouldn't touch it with a ten-foot pole. This is her phrase, but Lucien likes it, likes the way it sounds vaguely athletic, calling to mind the pole vault. What she means, though, is she doesn't want anything old in their new house. She likes modern things—sleek lines, blond wood, glass, a single magnolia blossom floating in a square dish. He has come to understand these things are classy, while Lacey's tastes were not. He has enough money now that he no longer needs to make a show of it. Simple, elegant, that is the way to go.

Under the drapes, he finds droppings. Mice, perhaps, or squirrels. Better than bats, anyway. Behind the chimney, he sees his stamp collection and then the boxes. Inside are bills, promotional offers, girly magazines he never missed receiving. Junk. He should dump the whole lot of it. Seeing it just makes him angry at Lacey—she couldn't forward this to him?—and what good is anger at a dead girl? He tips the box into the bag and dust flies up his nostrils and into his eyes. At the bottom of the box, there is a tiny mouse body, a baby, no bigger than his thumbnail. And he's crying again—what a mess! He is anxious to get home to Beatrice and a drink on their deck. He dumps the next box, and a thin blue envelope flutters out, lands on his lap. It's from France, from Jean. He would recognize that script anywhere—tight and curlicued like a woman's. The postmark tells him it arrived over eight years ago. He tears it open.

The letter is dated October 1937.

Dear Lucien,

How are you, my old friend? I trust America continues to be good to you—and why shouldn't it be? Who deserves it more than you? It was indeed good to see you and your lovely wife in Montpon last summer. Lise and I both found her charming. We only wish we'd been able to spend more time with you, but such is life. Soon perhaps, we will be able to see you again.

You have no doubt heard of the troubles which each day become more menacing here. Lise and I, her brother Alain and his wife, Esther, their child, Eugénie, hope to leave France. This is why I write: we need your help to come to America. The American government requires that we have a sponsor. Would you be willing to provide this support?

The letter continues describing Jean's intention to work as a chemist in America. They are learning English. Lucien remembers the visit in Montpon. He'd already made it big by then and wanted to show off a little—and why not? He'd worked hard in America and had a new American wife, though he understands now that Jean and Lise probably disliked Lacey— her big blondness and her laugh that became to him like water dripping from a faucet. But then, he'd thought she was his prize. He shakes his head as if to clear away these memories.

The letter has been sitting unopened in this stuffy attic for almost nine years. The return address is in Paris, not an address Lucien recognizes.

There were phone calls that fall, he remembers now. He knew even then it was Lacey, knew from the way the phone rang and rang, but did he answer? No, he and Bea had rolled their eyes, continued mixing drinks, making love, whatever it was they'd been doing. He had assumed she was calling to beg him to return, to reconsider, but maybe she wanted to tell him about the letter. Digging through the garbage bag, he finds another letter dated 1941. This one from the south of France.

Dear Lucien,

I hope this letter finds you well. I haven't heard from you in some time and thought you might have tried communicating with us in Paris where we can no longer stay. I write from Marseille where I am engaged as a confectioneur, *a challenging position at present given the sugar rationing.*

We remain intent on leaving France for America. I hope you can see clear to helping us in this endeavor. Perhaps I did not make myself clear in the last letter, but we have money for our passage. We need only your signature that indicates your willingness to sponsor us. Enclosed are the addresses where a letter must be sent. I include my mother's address in Montpon, though surely you have not forgotten that—and all our good times there together.

There are no more letters after this one, though Lucien goes through the bag, shaking out magazines, checking and rechecking. They were alive five years ago. Lacey is gone, but perhaps he can still save Jean. In his head he drafts his response to Jean, but it is difficult to explain the delay without getting into this mess—his affair with Bea, Lacey's anger and sadness, her death—and he wants the future to be free of all this.

It's late when he finishes at Lacey's. Everything to throw out is bagged and at the curb. The furniture can be sold with the house. He has already told the realtor this. Lucien pats his chest, checking again that the letters are still in his jacket pocket. Yes, he is all set. He drives fast down Alameda, the night air blowing moist and thick through the open windows. If he weren't in such a hurry, so bent on rectifying the past, he might notice Tiny, the famous trained dog, just a blur of white darting behind a pink house on the corner of Santa Barbara and Alameda.

IN FRANCE, JEAN HAS almost given up. Before the war, he wrote his friend, Lucien, and then again afterward—a careful, obsequious letter of which he is a bit ashamed. He has tried to reach him through the American Consulate, but the bureaucrats pride themselves on being unhelpful, on how much they can withhold. Lucien's first wife, Chantal, is no help either. "If you find the bastard," she says, "tell him I haven't forgotten the money he owes me." And this after Jean tracked her down for weeks. The end of the war has meant upheaval, just as the onset of the war did. This is the only certainty now. He stands at the bridge looking down at the gray waves of the Seine. The sky is gray, too, the color of paste. Staying in France is impossible. Here, resentments and bad memories clutter his days, crowd his dreams. He and Lise have already pinned the future elsewhere.

When Jean last saw him, Lucien had grown a belly that he patted with both hands while they talked. Jean remembers Lacey's red lacquered nails stroking Lucien's arm and his face as he spoke of the money to be made in America. She was a nitwit, but what should he care about Lucien's taste in women? Perhaps Lucien felt snubbed when Jean refused to join them the next night; perhaps that is why he doesn't write. Jean would sit gladly through a million dinners with Lucien and Lacey, he'd look at the publicity photos of their dog, and the three of them costumed, Lucien in a top hat and the wife in sequins, though who saw those things on the radio? Tell me again about the sunshine, he'd say, and the beaches, the way you can reach up and pluck an orange from the tree in your backyard.

But here's the thing: his waiting and wanting cannot stay pure, wholehearted for long. It begins to turn as milk will, left too long out of refrigeration. Wine to vinegar. He begins to find fault with America. How ridiculous are their big cars, how flavorless the cigarettes from the American servicemen, and how like overgrown children they are. Someone offers him American cheese, and he thinks it's a practical joke. Who would call such a thing food?

Still, when Lucien's letter arrives, it is cause for celebration.

April 3, 1946

Dear Jean,

Events conspired against my receiving your letters until now. I am, it goes without saying, deeply sorry I could not help sooner. Naturally, I am willing to do whatever I can to help you and your family. Money is no problem. I have written to the consulate and indicated my willingness to sponsor you. I was informed by the offices there about the deaths of your brother-in-law and his wife. Please accept my sympathy and prayers for you, Lise, and the child.

I, too, have some sad news. Lacey has passed away after a lingering illness. I am grateful her suffering is over and that she received such a moving farewell from her many fans and admirers. She was a good girl, who wanted only to make others happy.

I have moved out of the entertainment business and into manufacturing, a very profitable line of work. I have taken up the game of golf, and it turns out, am quite good at it. As a result, I am suntanned as dark as a Negro! Perhaps you will not recognize your old friend when we meet up soon.

I await your word—
Lucien

After that, new passports and visas must be obtained. There is much writing back and forth with Lucien, and even a phone call near the end. He hears his friend's voice—tinny and small; his own echoes back at him. Then at last, tickets are purchased.

THE SHIP IS A refurbished freighter. Perhaps it carried coal or iron ore, because there is a lingering dark film everywhere, and the smell of sulfur. Still, they are lucky to be here, moving steadily, if not rapidly, toward America. Lise and the child are ill from the choppy water, but Jean doesn't mind it after a while. He has grown accustomed also to the wet air, the spray in the wind. It is better on deck than in the makeshift cabins, where he hears the other passengers—children squabbling, the muffled grunts of lovemaking, snoring, even—he swears—someone picking their teeth. He is not alone in preferring the deck and has met a number of the other passengers by the second day aboard. There is a Belgian family emigrating to Texas, several war brides, and even now some returning servicemen and American nurses. There is also a Viennese seamstress, who claims to speak no French or English. She waves off conversation with rapid hand gestures. Jean occupies himself by trying to link the night noises to the passengers' inscrutable daytime faces, or he looks out to the horizon as if he can see there the future. Above, dark birds like a sprinkle of pepper disappear into the soupy sky.

AT NIGHT, A RESTLESSNESS seizes him. Jean leaves Lise and the child sleeping easily in their berth, and heads to the deck. He is surprised to find on the bench he has come already to think of as his, an American serviceman.

"Good evening," he says approaching.

"Evening," the man says, extending his hand. "Frank Samson. Pleased to meet you."

"Jean Latour." Jean extends his hand too, grips strongly. This is the American way, he has read.

"John," Frank Samson says, "may I bum a smoke?"

Smoke? Bum? His confusion must show, because Frank laughs and explains.

"Of course," Jean says when he understands. He readily extends his pack. The American takes a cigarette—a smoke. This will become Jean's line, his greeting to friends and strangers alike. He likes the sound of the words in his mouth, the casual, almost funny sound of "bum," the way the thing is reduced to its function. And smoking is a language of its own, a language he speaks easily, without an accent in any country. Yes, he is himself when he smokes, squints at the inhale, blows rings, flicks the butts over the ship's rail.

"Where you headed?" Frank asks, exhaling into the wind.

"California," Jean says. "San Francisco."

"Nice," Frank says. "Lots of hills."

"You?" Jean asks. Frank Samson has a smooth-looking face and pale eyes. He is young, perhaps 22, Jean decides.

"Tacoma, Washington," he says.

Jean repeats this, so he will remember. "Your family is there?"

"Yup, and my girl." Frank smiles broadly. "Haven't seen her in three years." He reaches into his back pocket and pulls out his wallet. He withdraws a photograph of a girl leaning against a fence. She has dark hair tucked behind her ears. She poses before a squat, white house of the sort he thinks of as American.

"Very nice," he says.

"I've been in the hospital in Grenoble recovering, or I'd be home by now."

Politeness and ignorance—he will not understand what Frank has to say about his illness—combine to prevent Jean from asking more. He nods.

Frank Samson lifts his pant leg to his knee, revealing a prosthetic. The waxy pink color reminds Jean of a doll Eugénie used to have.

"This here is a little souvenir of the war," Frank says. He looks out at the water.

Jean follows his gaze. Far away, he can see the lights of another boat.

"You were hurt fighting?" Jean asks.

"And then infection set in," Frank says. "Haven't told my girl about the peg leg." He raps his leg with his knuckles.

A mistake, Jean thinks, but he wouldn't say so even if he had the right words.

THE NEXT TIME HE sees Private Samson, he's in the dining room sitting very near one of the war brides, Suzanne, the one with the overbite from Toulouse. Jean is with the child, who, having established her sea legs, is ravenous. She takes slice after slice of the doughy white bread. Jean can tolerate it only toasted black. It tastes like glue, he tells her, but she only smiles, butter streaking her chin and cheeks.

"See you on deck tonight?" Frank calls out.

Jean nods, pleased.

That night, Lise reaches for him after the child is asleep. "Are you coming to bed?" she asks. She smiles up at him.

Jean shakes his head, pretends not to understand that she is asking if he wants to make love. "I'm not tired yet," he says. "I think I'll walk for a bit."

All through the war, when there was no guarantee of a future, he found comfort in her body. Now, though the worst is past, he cannot escape his present worries. How will he support these two, let alone the child Lise wants, a son to name for Alain.

On deck, Frank waits, smoking. The air is damp, with none of the daytime warmth. Jean is glad for his wool sweater.

"There you are, you son-of-a-bitch," Frank says.

Jean has noticed that Frank uses this expression often. He understands it as a jocular term of endearment. In private, he practices this phrase, aims for the same jolly tone and intonation.

"I brought some cards," Frank says. "I'll teach you to play rummy."

While they play, they talk about the future as if it were only a matter of buying the right car for the hills of San Francisco. Hudson or Chevrolet? Frank plans to work with his father. He thinks he'll marry right away—"It's June, ain't it?" he says, and Jean agrees that it is, though he doesn't know what this has to do with anything.

BY DAY, SUZANNE WALKS the old ship. It's not the fancy transport she imagined as she waited for all the papers and approval from America, nothing at all like the boats featured in the newspaper with the first war brides sailing off, their arms raised and waving as they departed, but she tries not to see this as a harbinger. It is impossible to pace in her tiny compartment, so she writes letters home. There is no way to mail them before she reaches her destination, but she writes nonetheless.

May 29, 1947

Dear Maman,

    I miss you already. I can't believe I've traded you and Papa, Lisabette, Arnaud, Michael, Sabine, and all the others for America. Tonight it seems like an unfair barter. But I am sea sick and lonely and that will all change soon, n'est-ce pas?

    All my love,
    Your Suzanne

May 30, 1947

Dear Maman and Papa, Lisabette and Arnaud,

    The boat is full of interesting people. There is a family from Le Puy, another moving to Texas to become real cowboys. The soldiers are all gentlemen.

    Kisses,
    Suzanne

June 7, 1947

Chers Tous,

> *The sea is as smooth as silk today. I feel almost as calm about my future. I've been too busy to write much and soon we will reach America.*
> *All my love,*
> *Suzanne*

With increasing frequency, when Frank joins Jean on deck, he stinks of Suzanne's perfume—lily-of-the-valley or lilac, something which makes Jean's eyes water. "She's afraid," Frank says by way of apology, though Jean wouldn't object. "I don't think she knows what she's gotten herself into with her fellow." While the boat hums towards America, Suzanne's fear and nervous anticipation seep into Jean: *What have we gotten ourselves into?*

LISE AND JEAN LIKE to rest after the midday meal, so Eugénie is on her own. Once the captain took her into the steering room and let her try the wheel. Another time, by the dining hall, the Viennese lady offered her the use of her binoculars. Mostly, though, she strolls the deck, feels the sun on her face. Eugénie likes Frank Samson and his girlfriend Suzanne. When she sees them sunning on the deck, they call her over. "Good afternoon," she says carefully.

"Hiya, Eugénie," Suzanne says. "That is what Frankie taught me to say—'Hiya.' It's cute, no?"

"Hiya," Eugénie repeats.

Suzanne's black maillot is studded with rhinestones. When she leans forward to talk, the top of her pale breasts puff over the edge.

"Hey, kiddo," Frank says. From his pocket, he extracts a stick of Wrigley's gum and offers it to Eugénie.

"Thank you," she says, but it comes out "tank you." She sits down next to Suzanne, who shifts to make room on the bench.

Suzanne has her American magazines with her, the pages marked where she has found recipes or hairstyles she likes. She has shown Eugénie her favorite movie stars—Betty Grable, Margaret O'Brien, Judy Garland. "Look here," she says, pointing to a picture of a yellow kitchen. "I will have a kitchen as pretty as this," she says.

Something about the dreamy quality of Suzanne's voice, lulls Eugénie, makes her think of her father. She imagines him waiting for her at a table in a sunny kitchen like the one Suzanne likes. "My darling girl," he will say. "How I have missed you!"

"She needs a nickname, Frankie," Suzanne says.

"Eugénie is a mouthful," he says, smiling. "What about Genny?"

"Yes!" Suzanne says, clapping.

"Genny," Eugénie says, trying it out.

"Then we're all set," Frank says. He puts his arm around Suzanne. Together, they beam at Eugénie as if she is theirs.

"Genny," she says again. It sounds perky and upbeat like the names of Suzanne's movie stars.

She is able to explain her new name to Lise and Jean by imitating the nasally way Americans say her name. Jean laughs, tells her she has it exactly right. This goes easier than she expected. Much later, she will recall that her father chose her name. The story is that he looked at her newborn face and decided: Eugénie. But by then, there is no going back.

IT IS NEAR THE end of the journey that Jean lights upon his approach to all things American. While they wait to be served dinner in the dining hall, Eugénie watches him spin the round tray in the center of the table. He takes the small bowl of red sauce, the one the Americans call *catsup*, and smirking, pours some into her drinking glass and then into his own. At first no one notices. Outside the weather has turned nice and everyone is cheered by the spotting of land in the distance.

"Oh, my," says one of the American nurses. "That isn't for drinking." She laughs.

"Oh, so it is a soup," Jean says, reaching for his soup spoon. "You must pardon me."

"No, no," she says. "It's a sauce for putting on meats or eggs. Some people like it on sandwiches."

"This," he says loudly, to get the attention of the next table, "is a sauce?" He nudges Eugénie. "A sauce?" he says.

Eugénie slides down in her chair. Against the cool metal back, she feels the heat of her sunburned shoulders. The people at the surrounding tables have turned and are watching Jean.

"You must excuse," he says. "I know sauces like hollandaise, béarnaise." He shakes his head, pretending puzzlement. "This is a sauce."

From several tables over, the American serviceman Frank Samson calls out "Welcome to America!"

Jean will do variations of this routine with other American foods and customs. Jell-O, for instance, he will find especially offensive and therefore inspiring. Even many years later when people tell him to have a good day, he will assume a serious face and say, "Thank you, but I have other plans." Eugénie sees from the first what he is doing. It is a way to stick it to them without appearing to. Behind the jokes and puns, the intentional mispronunciations, there is something unforgiving, hard, and bitter.

OVER THE PA, THE captain has announced they will dock in Galveston this afternoon. The noon meal is served early. The dining hall bustles with the women in their departure clothes, everyone combed and brushed and giddy with the thought of solid ground. After lunch, Jean tells her to run to their berth and get his camera, which they have forgotten in their excitement. He takes pictures of the boat, of Frank standing by the helm in his soldier's uniform, the brass buttons gleaming. Jean is posing her and Lise by the rail, when Suzanne finds them.

"Take one of us together," Suzanne says, reaching for Frank. Frank picks her up and pretends to toss her overboard.

"Stop it!" she shrieks, clutching her burgundy pinwheel hat, an expensive one bought in Paris for this trip. She has told Eugénie that it cost a week's rent, but she absolutely had to have it as part of her arrival outfit.

"Take it now," Eugénie cries. Her heart feels like it might flap out of her chest, fly off like the gulls above them. They are almost in America!

Jean snaps the picture. When Frank puts Suzanne down, they continue embracing. The Latours look away but not before seeing Suzanne's tears. The wind whips Eugénie's hair into her face. Frank places his hat on her head. Jean snaps this, too, and another of Lise in Frank's hat, Eugénie pointing to land until the film is finished.

When Jean takes the film to be developed, he is given doubles of this roll. He puts one set of the photos in an album, labels them carefully. He can't bear to throw the extras away, though there is no one to whom he can safely send them. This makes him feel as if that time is lost, irretrievable, though he knows, certainly he does, that time is like that, moving only forward despite our wishes.

IN GALVESTON, EUGÉNIE SEES Suzanne run down the gangplank and into the arms of a man with a mustache. Her pinwheel hat falls off as she runs. "But?" Eugénie says, and is hushed by Lise.

"Come, we've got a train to catch," Lise says.

Eugénie watches as the man lifts Suzanne, spins her around. Her hat lands in the water, capsizes, but Suzanne doesn't notice; she just laughs, her lips a slash of red as she and the man are swallowed up by the crowd. Eugénie cranes her neck, but doesn't see Frank anywhere.

TOMORROW, JEAN AND HIS family will arrive. Lucien has told Beatrice about Jean, about the pranks they played as boys in Montpon-sur-l'Isle. Without planning to, he changes some things—little details. For instance, as he tells it, it is Jean who is so poor, he must come to school barefoot, in torn short pants. It is he, Lucien, who protects and defends Jean from the other boys, boys who taunt and punch and try to fling open the school's outhouse door while he shits.

"So you have always helped him," Beatrice says, kissing his cheek. Around her neck she wears a diamond necklace he has given her.

Lucien likes this idea. "Bah," he says, "It was nothing for a friend."

"You're too modest, Darling," Bea says. "Dinner?" She rises from the couch and moves into the kitchen.

For a moment Lucien sees himself as he was—a skinny, dirty kid with scabs on his legs. What he thinks is this: when you leave your past as he has done, the job is never finished. You are required to leave over and over again. The one person with whom he might share this observation is Jean, but he can't very well do that.

WHEN THEY SEE EACH other, these old friends, the lies and guilt, the bulky pride and competition are momentarily suspended like the tendrils of heat shimmering above the parking lot. "I've missed you, you son-of-a bitch!" Jean says, setting down his luggage. They embrace, cry in each other's arms—loud dramatic sobs that embarrass the child, though she needn't be. All over the world, people have grown accustomed to such reunion scenes. There is the briefest of times in which this sort of elaborate emotion is tolerated, encouraged even. This is such a moment: California, 1947. A voice over the loudspeaker announces the departure of a train for San Antonio. Lise squints in the bright light, roots in her pocketbook for sunglasses. The child kicks at the gravel by the sidewalk. The men pull apart, look each other in the eye, and hug again, laughing now. From Lucien's parked car, a blonde beckons and calls out something inaudible, but it's meaning is clear: the moment is over. Their new life awaits.

HEIRLOOMS

T HEY LEFT BEHIND FURNITURE. Of course, it was too bulky, too big to bring to America. Out of the question—the armoire, the walnut dining table with feet like claws, though it was at this table their destination was decided, their future set in motion. And it was here the child, Eugénie, did her schoolwork each night, its surface pocked with her efforts, the indentations testament to her diligence and precision. They left marble-topped dressers, bookshelves with glass doors, a settee covered in a geometrical print, Eugénie's bed where she cried at night, thinking her sobs private.

Her Aunt Lise and Uncle Jean's bed had been his parents', its headboard painted with posies by his mother. This they left for a friend, but when he came to retrieve it later that week (petrol hard to come by still) it was gone, stolen by the landlord's son and installed in the apartment of his mistress on rue Vincennes.

They left family. Lise's brother, in a mass grave in a town with a name like a howl. Her sister-in-law, the child's mother, buried in Saint-Malo. They left a trunk of the tiny embroidered dresses she made for Eugénie, and bloomers, smocks with scalloped hems, the stitches so small they were nearly invisible. One or two of these garments might have been saved, so small they wouldn't take up much space. No, it is better not to think in this way, Lise decided. Better to think instead "useful," "necessary," "indispensable."

They left Jean's mother in Montpon, the village where she was born. She, in black since the previous war, in the back garden, bent over her lilies. "Go on, then," she said. "Go!" She didn't want to cry. Afterward she prayed the rosary for them, her only son, his Jewish wife, and the child who wasn't theirs.

They left the bakery Jean's father left him. They left the wicker baskets of breads, the glass shelves in the front windows lined with tartes and cakes, the air heavy with sugar. Jean kept the recipes in his head, but in America they fail. Cakes are soggy, soufflés fall, meringues don't harden. Later they learn that the bakery became Montpon's first modern laundromat.

THEY LEFT FRIENDS LIKE the Laurys, the Gelas, the Moreaus. People who knew them before the war, knew Jean's gâteaux when flour was plentiful, remembered Lise's laugh, the surprising way it started out loud and then simmered on. When Lise was ill, Monsieur Gela drove his bicycle into the country and came back with black-market eggs. Madame Laury played the piano in her parlor, and they all sang "The Marseillaise" though it was forbidden, and "Au Clair de la Lune." Their voices rose together, Jean's hearty baritone guiding them. Photographs from these times show the girls smiling despite their many layers, their knees knobby in too-short dresses, the women's lips heavy with red. The men are all handsome, hair slicked back, clean-shaven. The word that comes to mind is *dapper*. They seem not to make men like these anymore.

THEY LEFT WORDS, PHRASES, a sureness with language. Their mother tongue. They left their names because they proved difficult for Americans. *Eugénie*, a name like a brook flowing, became *Genny. Lise* became *Liz. Jean* became *John.* For a surname, they took the child's name—*Latour*—so they appear as one, a family.

In America, they speak French together in their home, but in this confined space, the language turns reedy and thin, a plant growing without light. The child is glad after only a year to shrug off the last of her accent. She can, after much practice, manipulate her tongue to form "*th.*" "*The th*eater is closed *Th*ursday," she can say, "due to *the th*reat of *th*understorms." She is an American girl now, walking to Thomas Jefferson Elementary School with her hair in long braids, penny loafers on her feet. She passes the cemetery gate of their new city with hardly a thought.

The new language makes them miss their old friends, people who laughed at their jokes. In the new language, it turns out, they are not funny, only odd. There are other problems, too. The American habit of concluding a meal by saying "I am full," which in French means "I am pregnant."

THEY LEFT MONEY—ONLY A small amount—in a bank in Saint-Malo. They meant to close the account on numerous occasions, but it was in the child's mother's name. They had her death certificate, but not the proper guardianship papers to prove they were adopting the child. So many papers after a war! Is the money there still, accruing interest? Perhaps they are rich. The child thinks of this money for many years, thinks of what it could buy her—crinolines like those of her classmates, a stucco house with an oval swimming pool.

THEY LEFT BOOKS ABOUT history and politics, songbooks, novels, several journals containing sketches and notes. They left the child's schoolbooks and report cards, a book she won for high marks—about the Queen of England, of all things. They left an old address book filled with the names of people they realized they never really knew.

THEY LEFT THE SOUND of *cathédrale* bells and their reverberations through the narrow cobblestone streets. They left the chants of schoolgirls skipping rope outside their window, of mothers calling into the dark, "*À table maintenant!*" They left the thunder of boots stomping up stairs, loud knocks, shouts, and then pleas. They left this, but not their fear of the night, and an attentiveness, even in sleep, to the possibility of loss.

For a long time, the child looks at any new place with an eye to hiding. Under the kitchen sink? The narrow cupboard by the stairs? Behind the thick bushes in the park? One day she realizes this habit has left her. It, too, is gone. Still, when she looks at photographs from before, she can't believe she is that grinning girl, can't remember what it was like to feel such joy.

"SOMETIMES," LISE SAYS, "I find myself wondering where something is—an owl brooch set with turquoise eyes from my sister or a particular square platter. And then I know: It is gone." She shakes her head, laughs at her forgetfulness.

It turns out there are things that cannot be left. The very nature of secrets, for instance, insists that they be kept. The child savors hers like a smooth candy in her mouth. She believes her father is alive somewhere, hiding still. Perhaps no one has told him the war is over. Perhaps his journey home has been long and difficult. Perhaps he is waiting for them somewhere in America, his arms extended in welcome. Sometimes she is certain she sees him turning the corner, exiting the trolley, but it is some other man who only resembles her father. He takes the arm of the woman beside him, pulls their child into an embrace.

Lise cannot not leave her desire to have a child. It dogged her onto the ocean liner and across the Atlantic, on the long train ride, and from their airless apartment to the new house. All her life holding other women's babies, her eyes tear up, her throat tightens.

WALKING HOME EARLY ONE afternoon, days before they were scheduled to leave France, Jean smoked an American cigarette and wondered how he would ever learn to like their paltry flavor. He was alone on the street at that hour, the businesses closed for lunch and rest. His eye was drawn to a dark alley where papers fluttered in a down draft. As he drew nearer, he saw that the paper was money. The wind made it lift and soar, spiraling back down to rest near his feet. He scooped it up, stuffed it in his pockets, but couldn't fit it all in—there was so much! He wasn't far from home, and he ran there to get a box or a bag. Inside, he pulled the money from his pockets, started to call for Lise and the child. The bills, he saw then, were old and funny looking. He looked carefully and saw that it was money printed during the French Revolution. The edges were crumbled and torn. He could buy nothing with this. Later, he took the bills to an antique shop and found they were worth little; they were not even pretty to look at, printed as they were in accordance with the revolutionaries' utilitarian ideas.

It was a silly thing to take when so much else was discarded or given away or sold. What will he ever do with it? Still, he cannot forget the way the bills sailed in the wind, how he felt running toward them, hope lodged in his throat.

A HANDBOOK OF AMERICAN IDIOMS

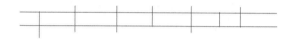

I. Raining Cats and Dogs

SINCE MAY, JEAN HAS been developing a shampoo in their basement. Through the floor, Lise can hear them in the basement. First there is Eugénie's bright voice asking questions: How much of the sulfate? Is she stirring right? Is it rinsed out entirely? And now what? From her spot at the kitchen table, Jean's answers are less clear, his responses most likely nods or demonstrations. There is loud clanging as he stirs the concoction in her washing machine. And then the water running. The basic formula was obtained from Lise's brother-in-law in Palestine, but everything is different here—the measurements, of course, but also the water quality, the proportions in the additives and dyes.

Initially, there were problems with consistency—it was too thick, which made it difficult to rinse out. Then it didn't suds enough, then too little. One batch left a sticky residue. In addition, Jean has firm opinions about color. He seeks a particular blue-green, a shade that will call to mind the sea in the south of France. He plans to call his line of fine personal hygiene products *Côte d'Azur Products*. But when the coloring is obtained, it turns the shampoo murky, an unappealing shade of green, more sewage than sea.

Before her on the kitchen table is her homework for her English class. She is to write a paragraph using the vocabulary from the handout the teacher, Mrs. Munro, gave them last week. This isn't hard for Lise. She likes memorizing the new words, piecing them together. Last week she got a grade of 100% on her essay about visiting the dentist's office, and in the essay before that—about weather—the teacher starred the phrase "raining cats and dogs" and wrote in the margins: *Excellent use of idiom.* Lise had heard the phrase on the radio, and it stuck with her because it was absurd, so implausible. Today, though, she is finding it difficult to address the topic: Where I live. She finds she cannot write about this place without explaining the other places, and there are too many, her thoughts about them too complicated for her English. She has written this so far:

> *I reside in San Francisco, California. California is called the Golden State. I used to reside in France. Before that I lived in Palestine. I reside with my husband and daughter.*

Below, something is knocked over. It thuds and rattles against the cement floor. Now Jean's voice is loud and clear, swearing in French, then English. When things go poorly, he is a bear. He growls at her, at Eugénie. Lise is holding her breath, she realizes, only when she hears the laughter downstairs, and she sighs with relief. Perhaps today is the day that Jean will settle on the formula. She writes her name in the top corner of the paper: Lise Latour and then her American name in parenthesis, Liz. She looks over her essay. "We are happy here," she adds because the paragraph feels bland, inconclusive.

Her class is held in an elementary school during the summer while regular classes are not in session. Lise fits easily in the children's desks, but some of the other students—the men and the tall Greek woman who never smiles—must hunch over the table, their knees up to their chins. Jean refused to attend with her, and after she saw the small desks that first day, she knew better than to try to persuade him. Oh, he would love that. And he is not a big man, would, in fact, fit neatly in the wooden chair. Lise takes a seat near Mr. and Mrs. Wu. They have lived here six months, longer than Lise. While they know much vocabulary, their pronunciation is poor. Mrs. Munro's expressive brows come together in a sharp V when either of the Wus speak. In addition to everything else, Lise would like to point out, they had to learn a whole new alphabet, but Mrs. Munro knows that as well as she does. And her brow isn't knitted from anger but in concentration. Still, Lise looks around the room, at her classmates, all of them hesitant, self-conscious, and feels they should be defended.

As THEY ARE PUSHING back the small chairs and gathering their books and bags to leave, the Wus confer in their own language.

"Liz, wait," Mr. Wu says. "We want for you to come to dinner."

"That is very kind of you," Lise says. Mrs. Wu is smiling at her and nodding as if to encourage her. But Lise doesn't need encouragement. Dinner out with friends! It's like a chapter from their text, one that would no doubt make use of the conditional tense.

"You bring your family," Mrs. Wu says, still nodding.

"We would like that very much," Lise says.

WHEN SHE RETURNS FROM class, Eugénie is on the front stoop, drying her hair in a rare patch of sun.

"We're getting close," Eugénie says.

Her hair is glorious in the sun, it is true. It ripples down her back, dark and shiny, the sun pulling out glimmers of red. When Lise gets closer, she smells pine and citrus and something lightly floral. "Nice," she says. Eugénie has her mother's hair, though Esther fought her curls. Lise remembers her yanking a brush through her hair, pulling it back into a tight knot at her nape.

THE WUS LIVE NOT far away, but they must take the bridge over the Bay. At the entrance, Eugénie says, "Tell me when we're across." She squeezes shut her eyes. Lise knows she is remembering the temporary bridges built after the war to replace the bombed-out ones. There were no railings on those bridges. To look out the train window was to look down at the water far below. This is a sturdy bridge with thick rails.

The car rolls over the last bit of bridge and onto solid ground. "There," Jean says.

And Lise, too, feels relief. By her feet, is a bottle of wine. She doesn't know if the Wus like wine, so she has brought flowers too—pink carnations—and she can smell their peppery fragrance even without lowering her head to sniff. What, she wonders, will they have in common with the Wus beyond the need to learn English? Is this enough?

Mrs. Wu has prepared an elaborate meal with plate after plate of spicy, aromatic dishes. There are sauces for dipping and others to ladle over the meat and vegetables as well as bowls mounded with steaming rice.

"How do you find American food?" Jean asks.

Mr. Wu shakes his head. "We prefer this. More spice."

"Yes," Jean says. "This is delicious."

"But we are happy here," Mrs. Wu adds quickly.

Her face doesn't look like the face of a happy woman, Lise observes. Her eyes are solemn, her mouth a straight line. Mrs. Wu might mean relieved, or maybe satisfied, a feeling like reaching shallow water after a long swim, one's limbs still buzzing with exertion. In her expression, Lise sees that Mrs. Wu knows, as she does, how life might have gone another way, veered down another path—and so easily. The other life hovers near, hardly less real, but unreachable, too.

"You must come for a French dinner," Lise says at the end of the evening.

"Yes, *chez nous*," Jean says.

"We like this idea," Mr. Wu says.

II. Money to Burn

By the end of August, Jean has settled on the final formula. The shampoo is emerald green with a fresh clean smell, neither too sweet nor too astringent. At first, he packages it in small bottles and gives samples to the neighbors. He persuades Lise to take some to her English class, where she is careful to explain that her husband is developing this shampoo. She worries her classmates will think she is suggesting they are unclean, in need of shampoo, but they seem pleased with their gifts. Mrs. Munro claims she admires Jean's initiative. At Eugénie's birthday party, the favors for the neighborhood children are small bottles of the shampoo. Jean keeps a couple of bottles in his jacket pocket at all times, just in case. The park, the gas station—these are all opportunities to distribute samples, develop loyal customers.

After that he goes door to door, something unthinkable in France, but here people throw open their doors for anyone—the Fuller Brush man, the Girl Scouts and their cookies. If no one is home, Jean has business cards to leave in the mailbox or to tuck in the front door. The cards are pale blue with his name in green print. Along the bottom of the card there is a ripple of green waves.

It could be said that Jean's genius, his real talent, is sales. Yes, he understands chemical properties, and yes, he is attentive to detail, and his product is a good one. He knows that each doorstep is a stage, and he dresses for the performance in his good suit, a tie handsomely knotted, his thick hair combed back from his forehead. "Good morning, *Madame*," he says. The housewives of San Francisco's near suburbs, Brisbane or San Bruno, what do they need more, shampoo or the break from their routine? All day, he imagines, they are busy meeting the needs of others—husband, child, home. The women wipe their hands on their aprons, invite him into the foyer. If it's a hot day, they might offer him something cool to drink. Sometimes there is a toddler on the woman's hip or children sprawled before a TV in the next room. He mentions Eugénie then, her help in developing the shampoo.

It's not long before he is anticipated in certain neighborhoods. The doors draw back before he has even rung the bell, the women smile, their mouths carefully lipsticked. "You're that French man with the shampoo, aren't you?"

"*C'est vrai*," he says smiling, cradling a bottle of Côte d'Azur shampoo as if it were a fine wine and he a sommelier. "This is true."

He is packing up one Friday. It's near suppertime, and he knows this to be a hectic time for his customers. He hears a woman's voice from across the street. He turns and sees a thin blond, her arms akimbo.

"Excuse me?"

"I said, 'What about us?'"

"You would like some shampoo?"

Inside there are no children, but her husband, older, silver-haired, invites him to have a drink. "Bruce Carmichael," he says. Jean is still surprised by this custom, this announcement of self so early in a conversation, and then Bruce is telling him about his business—construction—and how busy he is, all those returned soldiers in need of houses, schools, shopping centers. "Let me see your map," Bruce says. He circles an area near his own neighborhood and another farther down the coast. "These people have money to burn."

JEAN COMES HOME ONE evening in late November, singing as he enters the front door. He picks up Lise and spins her around, then the girl. He has sold his entire supply of shampoo. "It's back to the basement for me," he says, "but first, I have some things for you two." New pans for the kitchen, a set of plates all matching, and for the girl, a bicycle. It's royal blue and chrome, shiny, with a white basket between the handlebars. "Thank you, thank you," Eugénie says. Lise thinks the child will become an American now, riding off all day with the neighbor children, returning home only for dinner. What do they do all day? Where do they go? She must find out.

"One more thing," Jean says.

"More?" Lise says, surprised though she shouldn't be. He is a man of extremes, either penny-pinching or expansive. When it rains, it pours, she thinks.

"Paints," Jean says. From a big bag, he produces a wooden box filled with tubes of oil paint. There is a palette, too, and an assortment of brushes.

How long since she has painted? It was before the war, certainly. She lifts a tube, burnt umber, then another, cadmium red, feels the cool metal, all the possibilities.

III. THE LAST HURRAH

All through the war, the child was surprisingly healthy. And now, in America with plenty of milk and meat, heat that arrives whistling through the vents in the wall, warm clothing of the appropriate size, Eugénie is sick. Pneumonia, the doctors say. She's been in the hospital several days already. How many? Lise isn't sure. Eugénie's entire 5th grade class has sent cards, which are tacked up by the bed. Flowers were delivered from Jean's friends, the Carmichaels. Mrs. Wu has brought some Chinese candies in a pretty tin. Lise sits by Eugénie's bed during the day, waiting and watching, listening to the raspy sound of her lungs as she breathes. When Eugénie awakes, Lise might read to her, wipe her brow and arms with a cool cloth. At night, Lise sleeps fitfully on a cot at the foot of the bed. She isn't aware that this is unusual, but she wouldn't care if she knew. She isn't leaving the girl's side.

Lise worries that this is the result of the shampoo. All that time in the damp basement, the wet hair. She should've said "enough's enough already. Let the child go play." Oh, why didn't she do this? Why?

Now Lise hears the child's coughing and she's wide awake. It's thick and ragged and goes on and on like a car engine that won't start. "Unproductive," the doctor calls this kind of cough, but the other kind frightens Lise, too, with its rusty streaks of blood, the sound like something is being torn to shreds. Eugénie feels hot when Lise touches her. "Sit up," she says. "Sit up so you can cough it out." Lise tries to lift her to sitting, but she's too heavy with sleep and fever.

There is a button she can push to summon the nurse on duty, but Lise dislikes bothering the night nurses. They blow into the room, their mouths set against crisis and difficulty. She tries again to lift the child, and again feels scalded by Eugénie's heat.

"Maman?" Eugénie says, blinking, her breathe brassy and hot. Everything is hot. "Maman?"

"I'm right here, *ma petite*. Right here, right here."

"I want my mother," Eugénie cries. Her eyes are open and she looks right at Lise. Her voice is higher now and strange.

Lise stumbles as if smacked. It is the fever talking, she tells herself. The child is not herself, but it feels as if Eugénie is calling for Esther. That's ridiculous. She was hardly more than a baby when Esther died. Eugénie can't possibly remember another mother. She never even asks about her. A relief, that, because what would Lise say? Her sister-in-law was not a warm girl. She was always nervous, even her happiness had a dramatic, high-strung quality to it. Lise thinks then of the waves at Saint-Malo hitting the ramparts. Agitated, the locals say of the commotion and intensity of the waves. But she can hardly tell the girl that.

The nurse, Mrs. Reynolds, comes then, hearing Eugénie. "She's boiling," she says. "You must call me when she's this hot, Mrs. Latour." She lifts Eugénie's arm and places a thermometer there.

"Yes," Lise says. Guilt rises like a fever in her.

"I can use your help," the nurse says. She rights her pointy white cap.

The cap looks to Lise like a bird, like those rude gulls by the sea. "Of course," she says.

"Ok, sweet pea," Mrs. Reynolds says to Eugénie. "We're going to wipe your chest and arms. There, there, isn't that nice? Cool and nice, yes."

Eugénie whimpers but doesn't fight. She's too limp. Lise places a cloth on Eugénie's forehead.

The nurse checks the thermometer. "104.2."

"It was lower," Lise says. She'd been hoping the doctors would send them home soon.

"This is the last hurrah," the nurse says.

This is not a phrase Lise has heard before, and it strikes her as wrong. She hears in it endorsement or exclamation. What is the nurse cheering for? The child is sick. And Lise feels sick too, sick and tired of conducting her life in this language with its tricks and traps. "I don't understand," she says.

The nurse looks up from her ministrations, hands Lise another cloth. "I've seen it a million times," she says. "The fever spikes just before it's finished. Like a child's tantrum. That last bit of temper flaring up, and then it's over."

Lise understands the concept, but surely there is a better way to say all this. Lise tries to remember if Eugénie had tantrums, but mostly what she remembers is her wide eyes, watching, or her thorough engagement with her books or dolls while they traveled or plans were made, as if she knew on some level that this quiet was essential.

"We'll give the aspirin some time to do its work," Mrs. Reynolds says. "I'll check back in a little while."

When she is gone, Lise rises, turns to the window. Behind the shades, the fog is a thick blanket. Lise puts her head against the cool glass. She can make out nothing beyond the gray. She wishes Jean were here with her. Though he is only a couple of miles away in their house, she feels it as a bigger distance. He is working hard, she tells herself, making their future, while she has been unaccountably pulled back to the past. As she falls asleep by Eugénie's side, she thinks of the colors necessary to paint the fog—white, black, cobalt, maybe a bit of ochre. There is some solace in the colors, something accurate and true.

When Lise awakens again, it is morning. She is relieved to find that Eugénie is cooler and her color is better, less mottled. And she recalls her dream—or parts of it—her father was here, Esther and Alain, all her beloved dead gathered with her. It is a small room for so many, but everyone was well behaved, unified in the belief that Eugénie must be returned to health. And it seems she will be. Later when the doctor arrives on his rounds, he says he expects she will be able to go home in another day or two. He says a lot of other things, too, about rest, something strange about woods and a journey, but Lise hears him as if through fog. "Keep your eye on her," he says, leaving the room, and Lise nearly laughs out loud.

IV. HAND OVER FIST

The banker's secretary has installed him in a comfortable chair in an office overlooking the bank lobby. It's quiet except for the ticking of an impressive desk clock—silver and engraved to honor Mr. Howard Dorsey for twenty-five years of service. Jean didn't know there were rooms up here all those times he made deposits or withdrawals downstairs. It is hard not to feel he's been let in on a secret, been given entry to a club of sorts. And why not? He has worked hard without financial support from anyone—not Lise's family or his old friend Lucien, who is filthy rich now. Jean's books, which he has brought along, show his hard work. And he can no longer keep up with the production of Côte d'Azur shampoo. It's as if people really listened to his slogan: *ABCD, Always Buy Côte d'Azur!* He has intended to wait to move production to a factory until he has more capital, but Bruce has encouraged him to apply for this loan, that he, Bruce, will co-sign. Furthermore, Bruce's construction company will build the factory. He has a crew ready to go, the designs already approved by the city and the county. "What are you waiting for?" Bruce had asked. In this country with so little past, people seem to skim over the present, too, and focus almost entirely on the future—on the next day or week, the weekend, their vacation at the end of the year. This way of thinking suits him for the moment.

Jean likes the phrase Bruce used: *hand over fist*, though he finds it curious. He understands what it means, of course, but how it came to mean this is another story. He makes a fist with one hand, puts the other over it. His hands are worker's hands, calloused, knobby. They are chapped from the chemicals and constant washing involved in making the shampoo. He has old scars from the ovens in his father's *pâtisserie*, a knot on his right middle finger from writing. The nuns at *lycée* warned him he pressed too hard, that his letters were dark and cramped as a result, but he paid no attention. And now, he is in America, making money battered hand over fist.

This money, what does it do for him? Does he want a bigger house like the Carmichaels'? A newer car, perhaps a convertible?

He doesn't care about these things, or about golf club memberships or fancy restaurants. The money has made things easier. He doesn't worry as he did when they first arrived how to pay for essentials—clothes and food. Lise is able to paint while the girl is in school.

He has always invented things—when he was still a boy, there was a tart with poached plums, a variation on a village favorite, and later in Marseille, the candy cobbled together from what little there was. There is something about spotting a need, some gap that you might fill. It requires an awareness of human nature and desire and, of course, a willingness to fulfill them.

He intends to tell Mr. Dorsey his plans for expanding Côte d'Azur. He has begun experimenting with hand soap, another formula from his brother-in-law. He is considering making it oval-shaped with rounded edges so it will fit in one's hands more comfortably than the other bar soaps on the market. They're too bulky, cumbersome. Americans will pay more for less soap if it is easier to use, and of course, his soap will be good as well as comfortable. He imagines in the not-too-distant future developing lotions and bath salts, a whole line of Côte d'Azur products. He can see these bottles lined up next to the shampoo on a billboard, maybe with ocean waves lapping at them. Bruce has told him that he'll have to delegate matters such as advertising, perhaps even distribution now that the business is doing so well. But Jean likes being involved with every aspect, can't imagine that someone else would care as much as he or do as good a job.

He hears Bruce in the hallway, his loud laugh, and then he and Mr. Dorsey are in the office, and Jean stands. Bruce has clearly come straight from the golf course; his face is shiny and pink, though it's not particularly hot outside, and he's in his golf clothes—bright green pants and a yellow vest. The colors of children's clothes, Jean thinks. Even in this costume, though, Bruce is forceful. "Sorry for the delay," he says, pumping Jean's hand. He gulps the glass of water the secretary brings him and then launches right into his plan.

"Look," Bruce says, "this product, Mr. Latour's product, is a winner. It's already making money hand over fist."

Mr. Dorsey directs his questions to Bruce. It's true they know each other from the Chamber of Commerce, but it is Jean, after all, who is the real customer here. When he tries to mention his plans for expansion of the line, Mr. Dorsey doesn't look up from the paperwork before him. He slides the forms over to Jean to sign.

"Good job, Son," Bruce says as they are parting in the parking lot. Jean nods, but he thinks, my father would not wear the clothes of a child, would not play during the workday. He feels a flare of anger, not at Bruce, not really, but at his confidence and certainty, the ease that his money gives him.

IN THE YEARS AFTER Côte d'Azur's success, Jean will be asked regularly to speak to groups of aspiring businessmen, to college classes, an entrepreneurs club at one of the area high schools. Though an excellent speaker, he has retained his French accent. "On principle," he says when people comment. His English is good enough for that, for making fun. At his presentations, he likes to say, "For me, America is not the land of milk and honey. It is the land of shampoo." He suspects his audience remembers this quip long after they have forgotten his lecture. On the chalkboard or on an overhead projector, whatever is provided for visual aids, he writes this equation:

Good Product + *$* + *LUCK* = *Success*

Luck is the crucial ingredient, but nobody wants to hear this. If they hear it at all, they assume they will be the lucky one. Ah, youth, he thinks, can really make a guy feel old. This is the kind of joke he might have shared with Bruce Carmichael, but Bruce is gone. He died on the golf course,

115

after completing a full round, which is the way he said he wanted to go. Is that luck? Jean supposes so, though it calls to mind another phrase, something he hasn't thought of in years: *be careful what you wish for.*

V. Not Out of the Woods

The forests she knows best are the redwoods where the Carmichaels have taken them for day trips. She and Eugénie had wandered the paths cushioned with russet needles while Jean talked with Bruce and Jana. The painting must be of a forest from her past, though she cannot say which one or why it is so vivid now. Perhaps she is recalling the trip to Chamonix before the war? Or maybe it's the woods she saw from the train moving toward Le Havre and their boat to America? The painting is cool colors—blues, gray and a silvery brown for the leafless trees, as slender as fingers reaching for the sky. There are no people in Lise's painting, which is typical of a landscape, of course. There are, however, faint indentations in the snow, as if someone—a person? An animal?—was there, maybe even recently. It could be an animal, a deer, say, but perhaps there is a figure in the distance, among the trees or just beyond the painting's frame, a person trudging through the snow, lugging her few belongings on her back. You can almost feel the weight of her bundle, the cold air on her cheeks as the woods give way to an expanse of open meadow. The paint is too thick in spots, Lise thinks. Her efforts show where they should not, but still when she looks at it, she feels a swelling in her heart, surprise at her good fortune and the awareness—always—that it might've turned out otherwise.

WHITE LIES

I.

IN HER NEW APARTMENT on Tel Aviv's Dizengoff Street, Allegra Bobrov has finished preparing breakfast for her husband and mother and clearing up the kitchen. Newly married, Allegra isn't supposed to miss her work at the bank, but she does. At this time of day, the tellers are counting out the bills and coins, preparing their drawers for the customers. She was good at her job; the customers liked her, and she liked hearing about their businesses—ships departing, construction going up, the world whirring around her.

Not just that, she misses wearing her smart tailored suits and dresses and high heels. Seeing her feet in scuffed house slippers fills her with regret—and something else she can't identify. What is it? She tidies her mother's room, opening the levered windows to let in some air and light, though it's gray for September. Still, it's something, she thinks. She fluffs the pillows, makes the bed.

There are fresh flowers on the bedside table because Allegra cares about things like this. Even when money is tight, a single bloom can make the heart lift—and what's so bad about that? She is, without really knowing, directing this thought at the twins, her younger brother and sister—Lise and Alain—who believe her superficial, bourgeois. But that misses the point, she thinks. As she smells the flowers, a few petals fall from the yellow rose. She'll pick another one while Maman rests this afternoon.

There's a knock at the door, and Maman calls from the front room for her to get it. "I'm not yet dressed."

"Coming," Allegra calls.

There at the door is the telegram boy. Allegra steps into the hallway rather than asking him in, and later she will be grateful for this. He hands her a telegram and departs, his heels squeaking against the stone steps. The door to the street clicks shut behind him.

The telegram is addressed to Miriam Latour, c/o Allegra Bobrov, but Allegra opens it without going back inside. By its blunt brevity, she knows that her brother-in-law Jean has sent it before she reads his name. Lise would have put it differently.

September 30, 1944

With deep sadness. STOP *Alain dead.* STOP *Jean.* STOP

It's immediate, her decision not to tell Maman. No, she can't bear it. Allegra is glad her marketing bags are by the door, so she has only to grab them, slip on her shoes, and shout in her departure. She folds the telegram into her pocket and then leaves at a brisk pace as if she can outrun the news, the black cloud of it hovering about her.

Gone, her brother is gone. It is impossible to accept such a thing. For so long, he's been in France, that now she imagines him there still in the apartment she's only seen in photos, or walking the broad boulevards of Paris—far away, certainly, but not forever. Maman has been counting on his coming back. That was the plan all along—France for medical school and then home to practice, and now with the war nearly over, they'd been expecting to hear from him. But not like this. Never like this.

Allegra has walked too far somehow and passed the entrance to the market. She doesn't know where she is, the city grows and changes so quickly. The street she's on ends abruptly with a pile of rubble. She is sweating, though it's not a warm day. She leans against the building for a moment, wipes her face. She has to turn around and retrace her steps. What to do?

Jewish law prescribes such matters. The body of the deceased must be watched over until the burial, which should happen quickly. Then shiva, the days of silence and mourning, with family and then with friends—and all that food, as if chewing and swallowing were a way of grieving, and perhaps they are, reminding us, as they do, that we are alive, though our loved one is not. As for the living, their anxieties are to be eased, and isn't that precisely what Allegra intends to do? Poor Maman, she thinks. It's been two years since Papa died, that loss still fresh. To lose a child in addition is too much. Allegra remembers then something Maman would say to her when she was a girl and she was to mind the others, make sure they were quiet in synagogue or had their lessons done for the tutor, that no one was hurt or lost: "The fish goes rotten from the head. And you are the head." She hasn't been paying attention, and look what has happened. She will write back *tout de suite* to Jean and Lise and tell them that Maman can't bear the news just yet.

AT THE MARKET, SHE sees her neighbor Mrs. Kauffman by the butcher's. She nods and waves but doesn't stop to chat. Then she sees Madame Genet, her former piano teacher. Of all of them, Alain was the one with real talent, and she doesn't want to hear about that now, doesn't want to answer Madame's questions. Luckily, she is searching for artichokes and is pleased when Allegra mentions some nice ones at the stand by the cheese man. Allegra gets an excellent price on peppers. She'll make Maman's favorite dish tonight.

Maman is sewing by the front window when she returns. "You left so quickly, I didn't get to ask you who was at the door," she says, not looking up from her stitching.

"Just Mrs. Kauffman," Allegra says. "She wanted my recipe for soup."

"It's warm for soup, isn't it?" Maman says.

"I don't know. There's a breeze."

THE FOLLOWING WEEK, A package arrives from Lise. It's a birthday package for Maman, now many months late. Lise has sent a sachet of lavender, and the whole package smells of it. There's a drawing of lily-of-the-valley by Eugénie, her name printed nice and straight at the bottom. In addition, there's a card from Lise, an embroidered handkerchief, and from Alain, a letter. It is dated five months earlier, April 13, 1944.

> Chère *Maman,*
>
> *Just a brief note to tell you I am well and to wish you a happy birthday. I hope we will celebrate together next year. I trust your new living arrangement with Allegra and Benjamin will be pleasant. Please give them my love.*
>
> *It will not surprise you to hear that your granddaughter is a delight. She is doing extremely well at school—particularly history and math—and is, in fact, the youngest in her class. She will move up again at the end of term.*
>
> *We hope for peace and that we might all be together again soon.*
>
> *Your loving son,*
> *Alain*

The package is stamped so many times Allegra cannot make out the various postmarks. For once the mess of war, the changing borders and rules and governments seem to work in her favor. Maman is delighted with her package. She reads the letter twice with the magnifying glass. She pins up the girl's drawing by her bed, taking it down only to show to Mrs. Kauffman when she comes for tea. "Look at how fine her handwriting is," Maman says.

Eventually Maman will expect more correspondence from Alain, Allegra understands, but she will worry about that later.

FOR A WHILE, A certain degree of fudging works. For instance, a letter from Le Puy is written by Jean on behalf of all of them. And then, of course, after a war, one must expect delays and distraction—employment must be found, a new apartment, new school for the child. On Alain and Lise's birthday, Allegra suggests they send only cards rather than risk a package getting lost in the upheaval.

Of course it will require some explaining when Lise and Jean and the girl arrive, not to stay, as Allegra had hoped, but to visit before moving to America. Maman will want to know why Alain hasn't come, too. Some of this might be explained away by the distance, the expense of four tickets rather than three. Allegra is beginning to see the way her lie requires tending. It's a finicky plant, one that needs to be moved into the sun, then out, given just the right amount of water. Too little and it droops; too much it bolts, grows straggley and weak. Even carefully looked after, its buds might shrivel and drop.

IN TEL AVIV, THIS is what Eugénie is told: Grandmother Miriam is very old. The sad news would kill her. We mustn't upset her. This is for her own good. A mother shouldn't outlive her child.

"Do you know what it is, a white lie? A story we tell that's not entirely true, but it helps someone. You seem like a good girl—you want to help, don't you?"

At nine years old, Eugénie finds her aunt tall and imposing, elegant. Later, when Eugénie reads the phrase *handsome woman,* she will think of Aunt Allegra, her thick auburn hair, styled to swoop across her forehead. Her eyebrows are dark and straight and remind Eugénie of punctuation—exclamation marks or dashes. As soon as Allegra saw Eugénie's clothing—too heavy for this climate and shabby to boot—she took her shopping and bought her two new dresses and a pair of red sandals. Eugénie can't imagine saying no to her about anything, even if Grandmother doesn't seem so very old or frail.

Besides, Eugénie enjoys her conversations with Grandmother, the opportunity to speak of her father. At Grandmother's, sweets are often involved—halvah or baklava, sometimes a round cookie with a hole in its center that they dunk in sweet, milky coffee. She tells her grandmother how Papa takes her to school each morning on the back of his bicycle, for instance. How all the other girls are jealous because he is such a fun, jokey kind of papa and theirs are gruff, always scolding and forbidding laughter or noise. What else does she tell her? About the pony he bought her—Ruby—who is being boarded until they return, when Eugénie will ride her in competitions. She thinks Papa will marry again. He has four or five girlfriends and has asked Eugénie to select the one she'd most like to have as a Maman. She has devised an elaborate rating system that she describes in detail. She will have lots of new brothers and sisters after the perfect Maman is selected, she promises.

"Five girlfriends, has he?" Grandmother says, smiling. "But what about Lise, isn't she your Maman now?"

It's true that Eugénie calls Lise *Maman*. She doesn't remember another mother. She hasn't thought of this wrinkle before. Grandmother watches, her mouth pursed.

"I think I need the bathroom," Eugénie says, hopping up. In the bathroom, she runs the tap for a while and looks in the mirror, making faces, batting her eyelashes. She puts on some of Aunt Allegra's face powder, her lipstick. Maybe she looks a bit like Elizabeth Taylor, Eugénie decides, if it weren't for the freckles. Then, she's got it: They'll all live together—she and Lise and Jean with Papa and his new wife. It feels good to settle that, but when she goes back to Grandmother's room, she finds her resting, her arm flung over her eyes.

The next day when she's sent to visit with Grandmother, Aunt Allegra tells her she needn't lay it on so thick. "Just tell her about yourself—your best subjects in school, what you want to be when you're a grown up, your friends."

II.

In Daly City, Jean takes the Remington portable from the hall closet, smelling of mothballs, and lugs it into the dining room. The light in here is good if he works by the big window. He opens the case and removes the typewriter, which he thinks of as Alain's because he uses it only when he writes Alain's letters home to Tel Aviv. His own letters to Allegra's husband, Ben, are mostly about business and are dictated at work, and Lise handwrites her letters. In a file, he keeps the letters from Israel and a carbon copy of his correspondence so he doesn't repeat himself or confuse anything. Despite his care to detail, there have been slip-ups over the years. The newspaper article about Eugénie's award for the highest marks in sixth grade, which he'd clipped and included in a letter to Maman, mentioned Eugénie as living with her parents, Jean and Lise Latour. But Maman hadn't questioned this. Perhaps she excused this as a typo. Who knows, maybe she didn't notice.

Looking over his last letter, written on May 31, 1951, he sees he mentioned a conference in Colorado, so he can report about that. The newspaper has helped in the past, Jean recalls, rising to find the *Chronicle*. Yes, there are numerous cultural events which Alain, busy though he is at the hospital, would partake of—the San Francisco Opera, the Greek Festival, a benefit for the children's wing of the hospital—Alain would certainly be expected to be there, given his success in the field of pediatric orthopedic surgery, a field which Jean selected for him, in part because it required so much schooling and training. Maman understands that such matters would detain Alain, prevent him from traveling. Not to mention, orthopedics is a fitting career given that his twin was born with a dislocated hip.

22 July 1951

Chère *Maman,*

> *I hope this letter finds you well. We are all fine here—healthy and busy. Genny, who will not permit us to call her Eugénie even at home, has a piano performance next week. Now that her school is out for the summer, she practices day and night. I think I shall hum "The Moonlight Sonata" until my dying day!*
>
> *I'm just back from Colorado where I spent a fruitful week at the orthopedic surgeons conference. My paper was well received, and I was able to speak with surgeons elsewhere who are interested in the kind of work I'm doing. Colorado is beautiful country. I had the opportunity to get into the mountains one day and they were covered with Columbine—the state flower.*

Jean stops to light a cigarette, though Lise will swat at the smoke when she comes in from painting to cook. He crosses out the line about the state flower, which seems researched, false, as indeed it is. Instead he pulls the sheet from the roller, sketches in the flower using the encyclopedia's illustration as a model.

> *They look something like this, but alas, as if I needed to remind you, Lise got all the creative genes. I should have bought a postcard to include in this letter.*

He can think of nothing else to add. He taps his fingers. Sometimes, he's inspired, and the writing comes easily, and

124

while he's doing it, he's filled with good will and hopefulness as if he might see Alain walk into the room, as if things might still turn out differently, more to his liking. He doesn't forget the truth, not exactly, but it gets murky. Once speaking with a doctor at an art opening, Jean had said, "My brother-in-law is in orthopedics." And then back peddling, "I mean, he was." In truth, Alain hadn't determined a specialty before the war, nor had he been particularly interested in surgery. Jean had been glad Lise was on the other side of the room and hadn't heard.

Enough, he decides, and signs off. The signature he must hand write, careful to imitate Alain's light, slanted scrawl. Next time he'll write more. Maman never complains or asks for more. Alain has never missed her birthday, though he is less dependable with the New Year's card. Her responses have grown shorter over the years, and she always writes to all of them in one letter. *You will forgive me, if I only write one letter to the all of you. An old woman has only so much stamina.*

WHEN DOES MIRIAM BEGIN to suspect the truth? Is it when she first saw Lise after the war, so drawn and hushed? Is it the girl's silly stories? But after that, the letters come regularly—newsy and solicitous. And who can argue with a letter from one's favorite child, her only boy? Alain writes that he misses her, wishes he could visit but he's busy, so very busy at the hospital. She's proud that he's successful, respected, a devoted father. What more could a mother want? Alain claims to long for her *borekas.* He is a good son. Yes, he is, so why does she cry?

III.

Genny has been thinking about flowers, as in, shouldn't there be some? The wedding is a week off: June, 7, 1959. She has her dress, of course—tea length with a pillbox hat to match—and Jim has his suit. In the window of Iasiello Flowers and Gifts on

Market Street, she notes the display of bridal bouquets laid out on white satin. She's not having that kind of wedding—it's just City Hall and a few friends, but flowers aren't extravagant. Not even Jean can say that they are, though he likes to ridicule her wedding preparations. She finds the wedding announcements from the *Chronicle* by her place at the table, the brides' faces mustached or horned with red pen. If she lets on that this upsets her, he's only egged on. "You are so American," he says, as if this is scornful, but why have they brought her here if that wasn't what they intended?

She's about to enter the florists when she sees him, her father. He's about halfway down the block, walking alone. She recognizes his dark hair and his broad shoulders and the way he is holding a package tucked under his arm. Of course, she thinks, it makes perfect sense: he's come for her wedding. All day she's felt slighty off, headachey, but now she forgets her fatigue. She hurries after him, her heart beating too fast. She's grateful she's wearing loafers, because he's moving briskly. Should she call out? No, it's better to catch up, tap him on the shoulder when she's near. It's a rare sunny day, but the wind is fierce, whipping her hair in her face as she runs. Then he turns into a shop. Genny follows him in out of the sunshine. Her eyes take a moment to adjust to the darkness. Where is she? She would've followed him anywhere—an opium den, a brothel, or more likely and just as awkwardly, one of the gloomy Italian bars that line this section of Market Street, filled with men and smoke, but in fact, she's in Johnny The Ex-Marine's Shoe Repair, which smells strongly of adhesives and tanned leather, and no mistaking it, of feet. Her father stands with his back to her, waiting at the counter. There is an older couple behind him, the woman holding a pair of orthopedic sandals, the kind Lise wears. Genny could almost reach out and touch him, but she'll wait until he gets his shoes, until her heart feels less riotous in her chest. She's waited this long; she can wait another five minutes. Then someone—Johnny?—emerges from the back, a fine layer of something like sawdust all over his arms and hair. Behind him is a shelf full of packages wrapped in twine. Her father hands Johnny a ticket stub, and he turns to the wall and begins rummaging through the shelves until he's found the right package. He opens it, shows her father his handiwork, which is apparently satisfactory because her father takes out his wallet and extracts a bill. This close, Genny thinks her father looks shorter than she remembers, and perhaps heavier, but of course they were all thin during the war. Behind her, the bell on the door jangles, and a woman with a little boy enters. Her father turns then, tucks this package under his arm in that familiar way, but he isn't her father at all. He's just a man with the same walnut-colored hair, not even handsome like her father was with his high forehead and strong jaw.

"Oh!" she says, as if she's been slapped. "I thought you were someone else."

The man looks at her as he exits—an appraising, unfriendly look. Genny's face is hot with shame. This isn't the first time she's been mistaken like this. You think she'd learn. And just when she's believed she was done with all the scrambling, herky-jerky pull of the past. She studies a display of insoles and arch supports by the door to compose herself. There are so many things that can go wrong with feet, Genny sees, so many kinds of hurt. There are assorted bandages for corns and something called a hammertoe, and special wraps for bunions—all of them covered with the same sawdust-like spray. She squeezes her eyes shut against her foolish tears.

Outside, the man is waiting. He nods at her as if they'd arranged to meet up here when her business inside concluded. "This way," he says, bending forward slightly, almost gallantly, like a butler in a movie. Genny follows him, walking fast to keep up. They pass the bus station where a couple of grandmothers in kerchiefs wait on a bench. After that they walk down hill, past a small city park that Genny has never noticed before. "Where are we going?" she asks.

"Come along," he says.

Genny has been drunk one time—on cheap rum—and she didn't care for it—not the hilarity or the swimmy sensation. She'd known then that there were things she was meant to keep track of—rules and manners and basic facts, but they drifted off, tilting, like toy boats. This is how she feels now, too, and also as if some promise has been made, though she isn't sure by whom. It's humiliating to have to ask.

At Canyon Drive, he says, we're almost there. Then she's following him up a covered staircase at the back of a building. His room smells of burned cheese and pine aftershave. Genny takes her cigarettes from her purse, begins to light one, her hands shaking.

"No," the man says, taking the cigarette from her. "They're no good for you."

"Oh?" Genny says.

There is no more talk. When Genny tries, he shushes her, not unkindly, but there's no arguing either. He makes no comment as he removes her clothes, carefully folding her skirt and blouse over a chair. He indicates that she is to remove her bra and girdle herself and she does. He moves to the window and adjusts the venetian blinds so the sun comes in only in thin stripes and then he leads her to the couch.

With her boyfriends in high school, she'd endured the groping and rubbing, the tugging aside of undergarments to get at the critical spots. With Jim, it is more tender, but fraught—both of them anxious, determined. This is something all together different. She feels like a garment turned inside out. Her thoughts fall away, and all she knows is the ragged sounds she produces, a keening.

Afterward, she rises and dresses. It is a shock to find in her skirt pocket a receipt from her lunch—tuna salad on rye. It could be years ago that she left the stationary shop at the end of her shift. In the way a person might smack a shoe to remove a pebble, or knock against her head to get out water, Genny feels as if something has been dislodged, some hope or wish she didn't entirely know she held.

As she lets herself out and clatters down the stairs, she feels woozy. She is terrified that she will pass another resident coming up as she is going down and have to speak—even a greeting in passing is too much. What has she done? At the bottom of the stairs, behind a trashcan, she vomits twice. She makes it back to Market Street, but outside her house, she is sick again. When Lise sees her, she sends Genny straight to bed with a damp cloth for her forehead. Genny tells her she was window shopping, which is true, but also not, like so many things.

This is the beginning of a flu that puts her out of commission for most of the next week. All she can keep down is tea and toast. There is some talk of postponing the wedding, but Genny insists on going forward.

IN THE PHOTOGRAPH THAT accompanies the wedding announcement in the newspaper, the bride looks a little wan still. She and the groom stand before a hedge, smiling broadly at the photographer, Jean's concession to all this wedding foolishness. The bride doesn't carry a bouquet.

Out of habit, Jean is careful to clip only the photo to send to Tel Aviv and not the announcement, which mentions him and Lise, but not, of course, Alain.

BLOCK PARTY

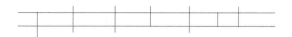

CERTAIN AMERICAN ACTIVITIES ARE still foreign to Magda West, though she has lived among Americans for more than thirty years. The potluck supper, for instance, or bowling leagues, their adamant church-going and now this: a block party. The invitation (if one can call the Xeroxed announcement that) appeared in her mailbox two weeks ago. Magda doesn't recognize the name and phone number for RSVPing, but supposes it's the new family, the one's who bought the Snyder's house. The block party is no doubt their idea, a way to meet the neighbors. Magda would prefer a tea, somewhere she could drop in briefly, bring her signature cookies in a pretty tin. She is caught up thinking of teas, of thin porcelain cups and saucers, sugared biscuits arranged on silver trays. The details are as vivid as if she'd just come from such a gathering, but it was years ago, in another place, another life. Annoyed, she shakes her head. Since Julian's death, she finds herself more and more drifting to the past. She is vulnerable without their shared resolve to leave the past behind. And it's only been two months since his death; her grief still new and surprising, the way it barrels over her, a train with many cars, banging and clanking against each other. She may, in fact, have to miss the block party. The thought of it

exhausts her. She takes the invitation off the fridge, stacks it
with the other papers she must deal with today.

When Julian was alive, they didn't speak of the past. It
wasn't something they agreed to do; it had simply developed
in this way. They talked a great deal of other things—their
work, their hobbies (piano for him, literature for her) and their
shared interest in bird watching. It was much pleasanter to
discuss the migration pattern of the cedar waxwing or try to
place the raspy call that sounded like a child's taunt. Could it
be the brown thrasher? The nuthatch? It had been enough to
know that someone else knew. Without him, she feels at once
that the past is lost and that it will overtake her. And there is
nobody with whom she might share this observation. Since his
father's death, Frederick has taken to calling every weekend
when the long-distance rates go down. But he might use her
admission against her. You see, he'd say, you should've told me
long ago. He'd pull out some of those hollow California words
and phrases of his: centering, opening up, authentic self. He
used to say "the universe will provide," and Magda had to bite
her tongue not to say, "oh, you foolish, foolish boy."

When he was here with his wife Keiko for the funeral, he'd
helped in Julian's study, settling the finances, arranging the
various papers. He'd found a key to a safe deposit box at Boone
County National Bank, and he'd taken it and gone to see what
was there. When he returned, he'd thrust an old manila envelope
at her. "Mother, what is this?" he'd asked. She knew what it
contained as soon as she saw the brittle paper of the envelope,
its red string and button closure, though she was surprised, too.
All these years, Julian had never mentioned it to her. She'd
burned the few photos, letters, and documents she had before
she left Prague. That wasn't her anymore. That was all gone.
The numbers on her arm she keeps hidden with long sleeves
year round, averts her eyes when she bathes. She might have

had them removed, but the process is imperfect, and who could she trust to perform it? She can count on one hand the people who have seen the numbers since the war.

"Mother," Frederick said, "who are these people?"

She had never seen the photos before, but she laid them out on the table and tells him what she can. This is Gerta, your father's first wife. This is their daughter, Anna. They were from Marienbad, not far from Prague. Anna, like Frederick, has her father's large dark eyes.

"What happened to them?"

"They died in the war."

Frederick had Julian's identity card and he opened it and pointed to the J stamped on it. "Papa was a Jew?"

"His family was, but he was a scientist. He didn't believe in that stuff—any of it."

"I see," Frederick said. "And you, are you also Jewish? Did you also have another family?"

Magda has always thought she'd answer this question this way: You are my family. And this is true! But nothing was going as planned. She felt dizzy. "I was married before."

"Did you have children?" Frederick asked. He is braced in the way he'd been when he brought home a less than stellar report card. Julian wouldn't shout or punish, but he'd shake his head. "It would be one thing if you weren't capable of more," he'd say. In those moments, she'd been sad for father and son in a way she couldn't have explained.

"Did you?" Frederick's voice was low, but pointed.

"Yes," she said. "Isaac was two when he died."

The name sounded all wrong here. If he'd lived, and come to America with her, he'd have become Ike or Jack, maybe Jake. This was dangerous, this line of thought. She stood quickly, and everything went black and fuzzy. "I feel faint, Freddie." She could've fought the dizziness, but she wanted him to see what this kind of conversation could do. It was like the walls of her house, the roof had been whipped away in a strong wind, leaving her in a pile of the rubble. Everything smashed, broken.

"Tornado," she said, recalling the name of the storm for which this part of the country is known.

"Lie down, Mother." He'd led her to the couch. "I'll bring you some tea."

There were no more questions that day or the next. He'd brought out a tray and some mugs of chamomile tea. He wouldn't interrogate her anymore, she thought then. And she wished she could tell Julian what a good son they had. "See," she'd say, "we must have done something right." Julian would have agreed. It was what they had made together—this child, his American boyhood, life in this Midwestern college town, far from that ugly past.

When Frederick and Keiko left later that week, he'd hugged her, though they are not a huggy family. "I have more questions when you're ready," he'd said. "I want to hear more."

"Yes," she'd said, but she didn't plan on ever being ready. It was too hard, and she was alone now, a new widow. She repeated the word, noting its old-fashioned flavor, a relic from another time. She remembers her grandmother, dressed in black, a tiny, bent woman, scowling at the world changing around her, though Magda must admit, there had been quite a bit deserving her criticism. She died before the worst of it, a blessing, Magda supposes, one that wasn't available to her parents, her three brothers.

So far, Freddie hasn't pressed her. In preparation for his phone calls, she lists topics they might address: Keiko's upcoming performance with the LA Philharmonic, the letter of condolence Magda received from one of Julian's former graduate students, the marvelous fragrance of her lilac bush this year, its extravagant blooms. She can mention the block party this time.

Waiting for the call, she sits before her wall of windows. She loves her house, the way it's nestled into the woods. In the winter, the leafless trees are gray and graceful against the milky sky, and now in summer, it's all green as if she's in a tree house, up amongst the birds. She sees deer from time to time, an occasional fox, raccoons. And squirrels, of course there are battalions of squirrels, like the fat one right now, scheming to get into the bird feeder. She taps on the glass. "Go away, you glutton. Scoot!" The squirrel darts off, but he'll be back. She must admit a certain admiration for their determination, their elegant, plumey tails.

When the phone rings, she tells Freddie that.

"You're getting soft, Mother," he says. "I remember when you'd run out there with the broom to scare them off."

She laughs. Perhaps the conversation will continue like this—jokey and light. "How is Keiko?" she asks. She can hear her practicing the Chopin études in the background.

"She's been working very hard on the Rachmaninov. She's not happy with the cadenza."

"When is the concert?"

"Still a month away. "

"She has time, then," Magda says.

"We were thinking that you might like to come hear her play, visit for a while," Frederick says. This, like the phone calls, is a new gesture on his part. She and Julian have only been to visit one other time, when he and Keiko were married five years ago. When she tries to imagine their lives in LA, it's like an overexposed photograph—the outlines of things are visible, but the details aren't clear or crisp. Freddie does something with computers. Keiko has her piano. Who are their friends? What do they eat for dinner?

"I would love that, Freddie. Thank you." She will need to shift some appointments at the office. Her patients will understand, and it's not like she does this frequently. After Julian's death, she was out one day and then doubled up the next two. This is what he would have done in her shoes. Yes, routine is its own balm.

When does the visit become an extended visit in her mind? And when after that does it occur to her that she might move there altogether? At sixty-seven, she isn't ready to retire, though certainly nobody would be surprised if she did. She can take the California derm boards and practice part-time there. She's good at tests. With that climate, there must be any number of practices in need of additional dermatologists, or she could start up her own small practice. She'll tell Freddie when this is all worked out, the boards passed, the necessary accommodations made. Everyone says that she mustn't make any big changes for the first year, and Magda can see the logic to this. It just isn't always practical.

It doesn't take long for the California Dermatological Board study guide to arrive in the mail. Magda could work in Julian's study, but she prefers the dining room. She can eat while she reads, though her meals these days are mostly crackers and cheese or a tuna sandwich. The dining-room table is placed before the windows that open out to the ravine behind her house, and the light is good here. When she looks up from her books, she sees cardinals, sometimes a warbler, lots of sparrows, all of them plumping themselves on her seeds as she fills herself with facts.

There is the matter of the house, of what to do with it when she goes to LA. She finds herself perusing the housing section of the newspaper, familiarizing herself with the realtors, pricing in this part of town. One Saturday afternoon after she's completed a unit in the study guide, she begins going through the hall closet, making piles of clothing to give away. She certainly won't wear these woolens in LA. She'll need to winnow and weed in the kitchen, too, all those dishes and appliances. And the bookshelves. She envisions a small studio apartment for herself—spare and bright, near Freddie and Keiko. She finds a box and is beginning to pack up hats and gloves when the doorbell rings.

It's Genny Horton at the door, a clipboard in her hands. "How *are* you, Magda?"

"Just fine," Magda says, irritated by the syrupy quality to Genny's voice, the look of sympathy on her face. "And you?"

"I've been roped into helping with the block party. We're trying to get an estimate for the burgers and hot dogs. Are you planning on coming?"

"Yes, I thought I would," Magda says, though until this moment she hasn't been at all interested. Two things have occurred to her: First, Genny's daughter, Sophie, might like some part-time work helping Magda sort and organize for her move, and secondly, the block party will be a good place to get word out about her house. Perhaps the neighbors know someone looking to move to this street.

"Great," Genny says, crossing her name off the list.

"What is your Sophie up to these days?"

"Driving me crazy, but other than that, not much," Genny says. And Magda remembers this troubling habit of Genny Horton's, this tendency to blurt her feelings in a jokey manner. It's meant to draw you in, wheedle similar confidences out of you, but she's barking up the wrong tree with Magda.

"I might have some work for her, helping me with a few house projects."

"She has been looking for ways to earn some money," Genny says. She looks at Magda expectantly. "What sort of projects?"

"Just some cleaning and organizing—things I put off while Julian was sick."

"I see," Genny says. She seems about to say more, but then remembers her task. "For the party, we're asking people to contribute a salad or dessert or side dish. What will you bring to share?"

"Dessert," Magda says, shifting her weight and stepping back to indicate the conversation is over.

"I'll send Sophie down soon," Genny says as she turns back toward the street.

Because Genny Horton is talkative and outgoing, Magda has learned all about her past. She knows that she was born in Paris before the war. The family pretended to be Protestant and moved frequently avoiding detection. "You know what that's like," Genny said, but Magda insisted she did not, that she couldn't imagine that kind of courage. Of her own past, she has said only that she and Julian met after the war and came to America for their studies. "But you're Jewish, aren't you?" Genny had pushed.

"Of course not," Magda had said.

UNLIKE HER MOTHER, SOPHIE Horton doesn't need to fill up the silences between them with questions or chatter. Her movements as she stacks and folds are quiet, never startling. Sometimes watching her work, her honey-colored hair falling around her face, Magda wonders what it would've been like to have a daughter, a sister for Freddie.

"What about this room?" Sophie points to Julian's study.

They have worked every evening for the last week and have made steady progress. There is a stack of things to donate and another pile to toss.

"Yes, let's wait on that one, shall we?"

"Ok. Should I make the signs then?"

"Signs?"

"For the garage sale," Sophie says.

A garage sale, another curious American activity. "Oh, no, I think I'll just have the Salvation Army come get it all." Magda can't imagine watching strangers paw through her things. And why the garage, smelling as they do of gasoline and garden hose?

"Let's have some tea," Magda says. "I've got some good chocolate too." She's glad she hasn't packed up the teapot, so she can brew them a proper pot. It's up on the top shelf. Reaching for it, her sleeve slips, revealing the last two numbers—the lopsided 8 and the seven, formed in the European way, with its horizontal slash. A button must have come off while she was working. Magda moves fast, shaking down the sleeve. Sophie is gazing out the back window and hasn't seen. Magda likes the girl, appreciates her help, but it's time for her to go. "I'm feeling rather tired," she says. "Let me pay you now."

"Oh," Sophie says, "I'm sorry."

"Now what do you have to be sorry for?" Magda searches for her wallet in her purse, glad she has her back to the girl. She withdraws two twenties and hands them to Sophie, more than she's promised.

Sophie accepts the money. Of course, Magda thinks, she didn't really want to spend time with an old lady. "Thank you for all your help, Sophie."

"See you tomorrow."

"Tomorrow?"

"The block party."

"Yes, yes," Magda says. "Of course."

THAT NIGHT MAGDA MAKES the pan of cookies she's promised to bring. The cookies are the first thing she ever learned to bake. A simple recipe, really, just sugar and flour and lots of butter.

She likes to add a pinch of cardamom. The trick is blending the ingredients just enough. Julian liked her cookies with a cup of strong coffee—just a touch of sweet to cut the bitterness. What would Julian say about the block party, she wonders. The cookies turn out nicely, the edges golden and the center puffed slightly. She has to retrieve a tin from the box where she and Sophie stacked them. She'll cut the cookies into squares in the morning after they've had time to cool. She lines the tin with wax paper, then wipes down the counters, thinking of California. Keiko and Frederick have never mentioned children, but perhaps once she's there, they'll see how they might manage. Who knows?

THE MORNING OF THE block party the thermostat reads ninety-two at 9 A.M. The newspaper promises humidity and Magda felt it just retrieving the paper from her front step—the air is as thick and moist as pudding. She's glad she baked last night so she won't have to heat up the kitchen. She takes the newspaper and her coffee and toast to the dining room but finds she isn't hungry. The heat has apparently made her birds sluggish, too; there is little activity by the feeder, no songs. She dresses in a cotton shirtwaist dress, stockings and her T-strap wedges. She can roll up the sleeves of her dress twice without revealing her numbers. Her sun hat is on the bench by the front door as is the basket of sunscreen samples she plans to distribute. She can hear people setting up for the party, and she hopes Freddie calls soon. It's two hours earlier in California, but still he usually calls by now. What if something has happened? There could have been a car wreck. What if he's in the hospital? At 11:30 the phone rings.

"Oh, Freddie, I was starting to worry," she says. The relief is replaced quickly with annoyance. "You know I have the block party today."

"I didn't realize you were so eager to get there." Freddie laughs.

"I had to promise I'd attend. And bring a dessert, too," she says. "But never mind, I'll go in a little while. How are you?"

"I've been talking with a rabbi at the Reform temple. Rabbi Berger is his name."

"Why would you do that?"

"Because I'm curious about our religion."

"It's not our religion. Not mine or your father's." Her voice sounds strange to her, but she can't stop. "I never believed in that. In any of that."

"Still, we are Jewish," Frederick says.

"Who decides these things? Not you, not Hitler. I'm not Jewish."

"Calm down, Mother. I'm just learning about it. I'm not becoming a rabbi—or even attending regularly."

Magda's heart is beating furiously in her chest, and she feels too warm, heat sweeping through her. It's as if she's been caught, called before her classmates, called all those awful names: Kike, Yid, Heeb, dirty Jew. And her best friend, Liesl, her blond braid down her back, turning away, joining a cluster of other girls.

Frederick is saying something about repression and grief. "Yes," Magda says, but she's thinking of Liesl, of a certain cookie her mother made, covered in powdered sugar, a dab of raspberry jam in its center. The way they gorged themselves on those cookies, sitting on Liesl's balcony overlooking Wenceslas Square. What became of Liesl, she wonders.

"I thought it was my fault," Frederick says.

"What are you talking about?"

"Your sadness." Frederick says. "I thought you and Papa were sad because of me."

"Freddie, no," she says. "You were our joy." This is true, though she knows she was not what anyone would call a joyful mother. She worried about illness, about injury, about grades. The whole of his life, a step-stone path of worry leading her somehow to this moment.

"When you weren't at work, you were always resting, laying down."

This is not the way she was, is it? She wishes for Julian's help. "We only wanted to protect you," she says. Does she feel a flicker of anger here, at Julian? Is that what this feeling is? Why did he keep the photos? Why did he not tell her? And why has he left her alone to sort all this out?

"Rabbi Berger says many survivors feel guilty."

What a relief to say that it's time for the block party. She doesn't want to discuss her guilt—real or assumed. She has grown averse to Rabbi Berger, his very name. "I really must go, Freddie." She hangs up before he can say anything else.

Her hands shake as she cuts the cookies and lifts them from the pan, but she manages without breaking any. She focuses on making neat layers in the tin, folding the waxed paper just so, but this thought slips in: She can't go to California. She thinks for a moment of getting back in her bed, skipping the party, but what if Freddie calls back? Or Genny Horton takes it upon herself to check in on her? No, better to stick with the plan. She puts on her wide-brimmed straw hat and sunglasses, swipes lipstick on, and sets out for the block party.

Pin Oak Court is a short street, really just a block, ending in a steeply angled cul-de-sac before Magda's house. Behind the houses on the left side of the street, Hinkson Creek meanders over a rocky bed, eventually meeting up with Perche Creek and then flowing into the Missouri River. How has she come to be here, ascending Pin Oak Court on her way to a block party? Her path has been meandering, too, and less constant, the current swirling, taking her in circles from Prague to Poland, to the D.P. camp where she met Julian, back to Prague where there was no one left, to St. Louis, sponsored by the Women's Auxiliary at Temple Beth-El. And then, here, to this college town in the very middle of the country where it was easy to be who they said they were. No synagogue here, few Jews. If they were asked about their accents, they said simply that they'd come from Prague.

In the middle of the street, a white canopy has been pitched. Tables and chairs are set up beneath it. Behind the canopy, she sees a truck with a long trailer. Two fat ponies are saddled up and tied to the trailer post, resigned. Their tails switch at flies.

She will just drop off her cookies and go home. How foolish she's been to think that this party would be anything but a chore. But as soon as she's at the dessert table, Patsy Bond is right there telling her how nice she looks. Patsy herself is deeply tanned. Her pool has been filled since April, and she'll be by its side all summer long, despite Magda's repeated warnings.

"But aren't you warm?" Patsy asks. Like the others, she is wearing shorts and a sleeveless top. The children are in bathing suits, hopping from one foot to the other, waiting for the slippery slide to get set up in the Pattersons' front yard.

"I'm fine," Magda says, "cold-blooded, I suppose."

"I'm going through the sprinkler with the kids if it gets any hotter," Patsy says. "I swear to God."

Jim and Trina Hartman join them after setting a platter of thickly frosted brownies on the table. "Hot enough for you?" Jim says, tipping his baseball cap to her and Patsy.

"And it's only June," Trina says.

"This heat is punishing," Genny Horton says, joining their half-circle. "Unbearable."

The Hartmans drift off toward the chips at the end of the table. And Patsy is talking about the youth group at their church

143

with Bob Langland, who still thinks after all these years that Magda's name is Maggie.

"Sophie appreciated the job," Genny says. "She's got all of the Juniors department at Golde's department store on lay-away now."

"Where is she today?" Magda asks.

"She's still sleeping. She'll be out before too long, I think."

Magda thinks longingly of her own bed—the good sateen sheets, her silky eye pillow to block out the light. Even Frederick's comment about her resting can't diminish the appeal of her bed.

Sue Teel comes over then and asks her and Genny to judge the three-legged race. It's not true that the other neighbors are all blond, blue-eyed. Genny doesn't speak with an accent as Magda does. She is wearing shorts like the others, but clearly people—and Genny herself—think they belong together.

"Oh, I don't know," Magda says.

"It should be fast," Genny says. "Come on." She takes the bag of prizes from Sue.

Magda follows her to the field.

"Throw the two single women together," Genny says. "Interesting, huh?"

"I don't know what you mean," Magda says, though she does. There are lots of ways one can be marked, she sees, set apart.

The finish line is in the empty field—the flattest lot on the street, but also, Magda notes, the least shaded. She pats at her brow with a napkin. It really is too hot for this. The races are delayed by some fracas at the slippery slide. Magda can't see what the problem is, but the shouting seems to be in German. How can this be? She squints to see better.

"What's the matter over there?" Magda points. But when she looks over the children are again taking turns.

"Just something with the water pressure, probably," Genny says. "You're kind of flushed, Magda. Do you want to sit down?"

"I'm fine." But she is starting to suspect she isn't fine. The canopy looks impossibly far away to her.

"Refreshment, ladies?" Bob Langland hands them each a plastic cup.

"Bless you," Genny says.

"Is beer okay, Maggie? There's orange drink, too."

"This is fine," she says. And it is nice and cold. "Thank you."

BACK AT THE CANOPY, the grills are going, the heat sending up shimmering ripples along with the smell of charred meat. People are piling their plates with food from the tables. She isn't hungry, but she accepts a plate and gets in line. One of the teenaged Berry boys is sampling everything at the dessert table. She remembers Freddie at that age, always hungry. She sees the Berry boy, Tim, is his name, take a bite of one of her cookies.

"What's in these—lint?" He pitches the cookie over his friends and into the trash barrel. "Two points!"

For a moment Magda thinks she might cry. Instead she starts to move toward him. It's wasteful what he's doing, not to mention rude. But then, she's stumbling into the folding chairs, falling. Over the clatter of the chairs and the pounding in her ears, she hears a child's voice loud and insistent: "something's wrong." Yes, Magda thinks, appreciative of the child's calm certainty. Much is wrong, not as it should be, beyond repair. Where to begin?

THE NEXT THING SHE knows, she's on the couch in her living room. A fan has been placed on a stool, and it's blowing cool air on her. It's still bright in the room even with the lights out. She hears murmuring from the other room.

"Julian?" As soon as she says his name, she realizes her mistake. Julian is dead. She's all alone. But who is that in the kitchen? "Hello?"

Sophie Horton comes from the kitchen. She has a glass of water that she sets by Magda on the coffee table.

"Dr. West? Are you feeling better?"

"I don't know," Magda says.

"My mother thinks you've got heat stroke. We're waiting on the ambulance."

"Come sit with me." Magda pats the couch. Her arm is bare, she sees. "My dress. Where is my dress?"

"Right there," Sophie says. She points to the foot of the couch, where the blue shirtdress has been folded neatly. "We needed to cool you down."

"Please," Magda says, reaching for it.

Sophie hands her the dress. "Do you want help with that?"

She has seen the numbers. Of course she has. And her mother too, no doubt. Sophie looks at her as if Magda is now someone else. This is precisely the reaction Magda has wanted to avoid. These numbers aren't her. They have nothing to do with who she is, but who will believe her?

Genny comes from the kitchen. "That was your son on the phone. He was worried about you." She hands Magda the glass of water from the coffee table.

Magda shakes her head. She doesn't want the water or Genny's care. She doesn't want to think about Genny and Freddy talking about her, their foolish conjectures about trauma, repression. Phooey.

There is a loud series of explosions then from outside. "Get away from the windows," Magda says. She gets up too fast and everything tilts again, goes gray and fuzzy for a moment. Her heart has started up its raucous drumbeat. Genny and Sophie stare at her, uncomprehending. But she, Magda, knows how to handle this. "Come," she says, gesturing for them to follow her.

"It's firecrackers, Dr. West. Timothy Berry brought them."

That rude boy, of course. "Firecrackers?"

"They're noisy, aren't they?" Genny says.

"Dangerous."

"Yes," Genny agrees.

The girl is nodding, too. It seems to Magda they have traveled far to reach this place of agreement. Her heart is still beating furiously from the effort. She thinks she might say more, but where to begin? Her fright? The numbers on her arm? No, the war is over. This is what she would say to Julian when he woke in the night, thrashing. *The war is over.* The sirens she hears now are the ambulance, not police with dogs and clubs. The medics will arrive and move her gently onto their gurney. Care will be taken with obtaining her vitals. They may start her on an I.V. Perhaps they will scold her about staying hydrated, out of the sun, all things she knows well. *Over, over, over.*

"Look," she points. A male cardinal swoops onto the feeder outside the window. He's bright red, as startling as blood from a new cut. "He knows he's handsome, that one."

JEWS OF THE MIDDLE WEST

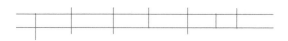

SOPHIE'S GRANDPARENTS ARE AMONG the oldest residents in The Pines' independent living condominiums. Next door are the assisted-living apartments with ramps instead of stairs and buttons to push in case of an emergency. And set back from these, an older building with white columns, the nursing home. "Going, going, gone," Jean says of this arrangement.

"Shush," Lise tells him, but she needn't worry. The other residents—mostly women—don't hear well, plus Jean's accent, thick still after all these years in the States, baffles those who can hear. "I can't understand a thing he says," their new neighbor Joyce Wagner says, "but I'm sure it's something perfectly lovely. Where are you from again?"

"California," Jean says, knowing full well that this isn't what she means. "But now we live in Misery," he says, purposefully mispronouncing Missouri. At first Sophie's mother had laughed at this, but she's grown tired of it; Sophie can tell by the way she presses her lips together. Her grandparents have only been in town a month.

HER MOTHER IS FINISHING her dissertation, her friends are away or working, so Sophie finds herself at The Pines, talking with her grandparents when she's not working herself. Their stories stir something in her at fifteen—pride and awe, and longing, too, though she doesn't know for what. The past feels more something—real? clear?—than the present, which simply surrounds her, hazy and gray. Could she be as brave as Lise and Jean were, as daring? She doubts it. At a pool party last year, a boy from her science class had said, "I've got a great joke. Wait, is anyone here Jewish?" And she'd looked down at her lap, said nothing. What could she do? Ruin everyone's fun? "Know why Jews have big noses? The guy had said, grinning expectantly. "Because air is free!"

"You do what you have to," Lise says of the past.

Sophie flips through Lise and Jean's photo albums as Lise talks. "Where is this?" she asks. It's a photo of her mother as a baby, her eyes wide and worried as if she's about to cry. Her dimpled fists are stuffed into her mouth.

"Paris, I think. Yes, look at her plump little legs." She was such a good baby, so good." Lise shakes her head, as if Genny is gone rather than grown up. Underneath the photo, Jean has written, "Eugénie, *six mois*." Her grandparents are the only ones who call her mother Eugénie anymore; she's been Genny for years.

"Later, Jean and Alain were stationed on the Maginot Line. It was the Phony War, and I got a telegram that Esther, her mother, was dying in Saint-Malo—far from Paris, where I was.

"I went to Esther, of course. She was very sick, her husband away." Lise shakes her head, looks back at the photograph.

"I will never forget," she says, "Just after Esther died, Eugénie, your mother, called out: 'Maman, Maman!' I went into her nursery," Lise says. "She was about two-and-a-half then, standing up in her crib. Such a pretty baby."

"I thought, she'll cry when I come in. She wanted her mother. But when she sees me, she just smiled and lifted up her arms to me, said *Maman*, again. So you see," Lise says, smiling now, "she adopted me."

Sophie loves this story, the way the pieces come together— Lise unable to have children of her own, Eugénie in need of a mother. There is a satisfying logic to this story, a rightness.

"What was Esther like?" Sophie asks.

"Poor girl," Lise says. "She didn't want to die."

"Did you like her?" Sophie asks. Lise and Jean are the only ones who remember Esther; Genny knows little more about her than Sophie does. There are few photographs of Esther, and she appears different in the ones they do have: Here, petite, dark, her features sharp, but in another, she is moon-faced, smiling.

"Have I told you about leaving Montpon?" Lise asks. She points to a photograph of a woman dressed all in black, her hair completely white. "This is Jean's mother and her garden."

"Tell me again," Sophie says. She is always hopeful that Lise will recall something more as she talks, a bit of information or a detail that will crystallize her sense of that time. Just last week, for instance, she learned that Esther was a seamstress, and now when Lise speaks of her, she imagines her bent over a sewing machine, straight pins in her mouth.

"So, the fighting begins, and I'm in Montpon with Eugénie."

"With Jean's mother," Sophie says.

"Yes," Lise says, tapping the photograph. "She was very good to me, to Eugénie. When the Germans got to town, they put up signs everywhere, demanding all Jews register at the *mairie*. Jean's mother thought I should ignore the orders, pretend I'm Protestant, but I knew I had to get Eugénie and myself out of there—and fast. So many people knew I was Jewish and if I didn't register maybe someone will give me away. You see, Jean had bragged about marrying a Jewish girl—me!

"So I left right away, first walking, then I find a ride. Finally, I got one of the last trains before travel papers became necessary. I had only a little money, not much food for the trip, not even a plan. We ran to Marseille, where there were no Germans. And almost as soon as we arrived, I hear my name: *Lise! Lise, is that you?* It's a friend from Paris and she takes us home with her, feeds us, helps me notify Jean and Alain. Lucky." Lise shakes her head.

"Weren't you afraid?" Sophie asks.

"That was a long time ago," Lise says. "But now, Sophie, I need to rest, and you go to work, no?"

DOWNTOWN DONUTS IS ON the corner of Providence and Ash streets, not really downtown at all, where the shops and bars cater to the college kids. Downtown Donuts is across the street from the city rec center and the public housing complex, the projects. Beyond that, there are some tiny houses with chain-link fences and plastic sheeting over the windows and a smattering of repair shops or stores that sell supplies or unrecognizable parts. Grubby, utilitarian places, their storefront windows open up to dusty interiors, stacks of boxes or pallets. Then there is nothing until the interstate, which cuts a straight line through Missouri.

When Sophie enters the shop, the smell of sugar and grease and cigarette smoke is overpowering. Most everything here is bright pink or orange—the counters and molded plastic seats, the logo on the napkins and the bags and boxes—too bright, as garish and artificial as the frosting on the donuts. Leandra is behind the counter, and the line of customers is three deep.

Sophie takes her purse back to the break room and shoves it in her locker. She slips off her sandals, replacing them with her work shoes. She avoids the mirror by the lockers, which will reflect back her pale waifishness, her hair frizzing despite her strenuous attempts to tame it. By the lockers, there is a yellowed sign from before Sophie started here. It says "Employes one donut one drink per shift." When Sophie first started working here, Leandra pointed to the sign and said, "I'll limit myself to one donut when he learns how to speak English." Mr. Yang, the owner, is hardly ever here, but it's Thursday, which means he'll be in later to do the books.

Now at the counter, Leandra is a model employee, moving briskly from the coffee pot to the donut case. As she moves, her blond ponytail swings behind her. "The Bavarian Cream are popular," she tells a tanned woman whose long hair is sprayed stiff in an approximation of Farrah Fawcett's. Sophie joins her, taking orders, filling to-go cups, snapping on the lids, throwing in sugar packets and creamers, pulling donuts from the trays. "Welcome to Downtown Donuts," she says. "What can I get for you today?"

When the crowd is gone, there is a slow stretch. Sophie gets herself a diet soda. Leandra is talking with the men from the neighborhood, the regulars, who intimidate Sophie when she's here alone, but Leandra jokes easily with them—Keefe, who has an impressive afro and keeps a hair pick in his back pocket; Murray, who delivers dry cleaning and sometimes comes in wearing his uniform, his name embroidered over the breast pocket; and James and Big James, who are cousins. Big James is actually the smaller of the two, but older by a month.

"We drank so much," Leandra is saying, "that when I woke up this morning, I was still drunk."

Keefe whistles. "Wednesday night. What's that mean for Friday?"

"I know," Leandra says, laughing.

Blond and suntanned golden, Leandra manages to look good in the Downtown Donut uniform, a shapeless pink and khaki dress with a faux apron. Sophie thinks about her own

Wednesday night; dinner with her mother and grandparents, a game of Scrabble in which Jean tried to use both French and English. Also swear words.

"Look alive," Murray says, nodding toward the parking lot, where Mr. Yang's station wagon is pulling in.

"Shit," Leandra says. "Glad I restocked already."

When Mr. Yang comes in, the men get serious about the newspaper, shaking their heads and muttering about Reagan. Mr. Yang nods at Sophie and Leandra and then ducks into the back. Sophie collects some dirty mugs from the counter, stacks them into the dishwasher.

"It's so dead today," Leandra says. "I'm gonna see if I can leave early."

When she returns to the front, she's changed out of her uniform and into jeans and a T-shirt. "I'm outta here," she says, "Y'all have fun." She waves as if to a child, bending her fingers to her palm.

AT SIX, SOPHIE EATS her one donut. She's working her way through the varieties. Tonight it's a sour-cream donut, which tastes better than its name suggests. She pours herself a coffee to go with it. Since Leandra has left, she doesn't take an official break but eats standing. It hardly matters since the shop is empty. Mr. Yang asked her to clean behind the counter. She's done that, swept the front, restocked the to-go cups and bags. This is when she likes Downtown Donuts best, these quiet pauses. Through the big windows, the evening sun burnishes the counter and stools. The air conditioning hums. Sophie sips her coffee and watches the cars and trucks speed past on Providence.

A group of kids about her age saunter over from the rec center around seven, and her quiet is over. Sophie has seen them in here before. The two girls, both in tube tops, go directly to the ladies' room. Three of the guys sit down at the counter, spin on the stools. The two other boys debate donut holes versus donuts. When the girls return, they join the discussion.

"That's what I like," the girl in the red tube top says, pointing to the glazed donuts. Her rows of braids are finished off with bright red beads that clack when she moves her head. Her fingernails, too, are red.

"Those are nasty," the other girl says. "Gimme a Coke. A large. Not too much ice."

The girl's hair is pulled back into a short ponytail, high on her head, like a crown. And it's clear she's the queen of this group, too.

At the counter, one boy opens a sugar packet and empties it into his mouth.

"Anything else to drink?" Sophie asks.

This provokes a hoot of laughter from the group. She corrects herself: "Any other sodas?" When nobody answers, she turns to get the drink. As soon as she sets it on the counter by the cash register, the queen snatches it and inspects the amount of ice, then drinks as if parched.

"Anything else?" Sophie says.

The tallest of the boys orders two glazed donuts. "I ain't paying for your Coca-Cola, Tameka," he says.

"I don't got any money," she says. This fact seems not to concern her.

"I got it, Marcus," says the boy at the counter, still spinning on the stool. "But she gonna owe me." He gives Tameka an appraising look.

"You'll get your 99 cent," she says, "but that's all you're getting." She shakes her head.

The boy hands Sophie a dollar bill. "Keep the change," he says.

Sophie tries to conjure Leandra's cool. "Thanks," she says, like she's in on the joke. "Ha ha." She fishes the four cents for tax out of the loose-change dish by the register.

"It feels good in here," Tameka's sidekick says, settling onto a stool. "Love me some A-Cee."

Rather than standing around, Sophie decides she'll get the coffee ready for the morning shift. When she dumps out the last of the old burnt coffee, the smell reminds her of Lise's story of making coffee from roasted barley during the war. They ate barley soup and barley cakes, bread. It kept them alive, but after the war they never ate barley again. She rinses out the coffee pots, sloshing the water in the carafes. She scoops coffee into the filters and makes sure the chambers are filled with water.

The kids' talk grows louder. Someone hoots. "What you looking at?" Tameka says, when Sophie looks over. "Don't y'all got some frosting to do?"

Sophie feels her face go red and splotchy as if she's been slapped. Before she can respond, she sees Marcus grab the other guy, the big tipper, and shove him up against the glass wall.

"What did you say?" Marcus is shouting. "What's that, motherfucker?"

"Woah!" Tameka says. "You gonna let him get away with that?"

Another boy tries to pull Marcus back, but he gets swung at too. Blood snakes from his nose, bright red.

Sophie has only seen fights on TV or in movies, and this is nothing like that. Here in Downtown Donuts, the boys' movements are clumsy, awkward, flailing. The grunting is intimate and awful; it's like listening to someone in a bathroom stall. Big Tipper spits when he shouts. Some lands on Marcus's face, and then he's pulled out a pocketknife. He holds it toward

Big Tipper, his face twisted and sweaty. Tameka makes a noise that could mean alarm or approval.

Sophie starts for the back, for Mr. Yang, but he's already heard the shouting. "Out!" he yells, emerging from his office. "All of you out, now. Police on the way!"

Marcus takes another lunge at Big Tipper and then thinks better of it. The girls are out the door, shouting back at Mr. Yang, "Ah-so! China Man, ah-so!" Sophie can see them pretend bowing, their palms together until they're out of the parking lot.

"Animals!" he shouts after them. And then looking over at Sophie, he shakes his head. "I'm from Korea."

"I'm sorry," Sophie says, but Mr. Yang doesn't seem to hear. And what is she apologizing for exactly? The girls' rudeness? Their ignorance? Her own?

The lights and sirens of the police cars bring people out of the rec center and the projects. Mr. Yang is sweating profusely, trying to shoo away the crowd, which begins to gather in the parking lot. The two policemen—both men with graying crew cuts—have more success in getting the crowd cleared. Officer Long questions Sophie, while the other policeman speaks with Mr. Yang inside. After this, Mr. Yang tells her to go on home. "Shop closed."

She gathers her things from the break room. She calls home, but her mother isn't there. Lise and Jean don't drive anymore. She'll walk. It's still light out at 8:00, still hot, too. She's hardly out of the parking lot when the police car slows and the window lowers. It's Officer Long.

"Need a lift?"

"That would be great," she says. "Thank you." Inside the police car, the air conditioning blows loudly. A radio emits blasts of staticky speech. Settling into the cool car, she can smell Downtown Donuts on herself—her hair and skin, her uniform.

Even her socks and underwear when she peels them off at home will reek of the place.

"Where to?" Officer Long asks, and she gives him her address. The car turns down Ash Street, passes the sad, listing houses, old couches crammed onto their porches and moves towards Sophie's tree-lined street.

"You got to watch yourself around those people," Officer Long says, not taking his eyes from the road. His face is shiny and pink, smug with certainty.

If her mother or grandparents were here, they wouldn't let Officer Long get away with this. They know firsthand how this story goes. They'd launch into a defense of the teens—the effects of bigotry and prejudice, the historic lack of opportunities for blacks in this country, the resulting sense of disenfranchisement. "It's okay," Sophie says, but she's sick of donuts, the grease-slick floor, the frosting all over her hands and arms, in her hair, the frumpy uniform—all of it.

"I wouldn't want any daughter of mine working there," he says, shaking his head. "No, sirree."

"Thanks for the ride," Sophie says, getting her house key from her purse.

Her mother pulls in just as Officer Long is leaving. "What was that all about?" she says. "Are you ok?" She's carrying a stack of thick books with both arms.

"I'm fine," Sophie says. "Some kids got into it at the shop."

"And the police were called in?" Her mother is pale from spending so much time in the library. She takes off her glasses and massages the bridge of her nose where her glasses leave an angry red mark. She looks both older and younger without her glasses. Bewildered and vulnerable.

"Just kids fooling around," Sophie says. "No biggie." As she talks she sees how Lise and Jean's stories might be like this—tidied up, altered to prevent alarm, certain jagged edges sloughed off.

IT'S TOO HOT FOR coffee and donuts, Sophie thinks. Too hot for anything. When she left her grandparents at The Pines, the pool was empty, the lounge chairs folded up, stacked in the shade of the pool house. Outside Downtown Donuts, the parking lot sends up shimmering heat. Only Keefe and Murray are at the counter, lingering over their cinnamon rolls and coffee. Leandra is in back finishing up some frosting.

"Get me another," Keefe says to Sophie, "would ya?"

"Manners, Keefe," Leandra says, returning with the chocolate frosted. She slides the tray into place.

"Please," he says, smiling.

Sophie has never seen him smile before, and she wishes she had elicited his wide grin rather than Leandra.

"May I *please* get a refill," he says.

"Is this your first one?" Sophie asks, remembering the new rules. Since the fight, new signs have gone up in the break room and by the counter too: "Free refill means ONE cup!" "Customers pay first! Then served."

"Oh, yeah," Leandra says. "New rules, gentlemen."

"Seriously?" Murray says.

Keefe shakes his head. "He's going to Jew us out of refills, I'm going to Ernie's from now on."

Sophie's face goes hot. She's never heard this phrase before, but she knows exactly what it means, to what it refers. There is something especially ugly about the phrasing: *Jew* as verb.

"Whatever," Leandra says, shrugging at Sophie. She takes the carafe from the burner and pours refills for both men. "I'm not going to sweat it."

"That's rude," Sophie blurts, too loud. To her ears she sounds petulant, childish.

"Huh?" Keefe looks up surprised, as if he's noticing her for the first time.

"What you said is rude," she says, working to steady her voice.

"What did I say?" He looks to Murray, who is stirring sugar into his coffee.

The timer bleats sharply indicating that the dishwasher is done and Sophie jumps. "Relax," Leandra says, laughing. "It's not a gunshot."

"I'll get it," Sophie says, turning away. What a relief to have a task, something to get her away from the counter, this conversation, from Keefe who has added so much cream and sugar to his coffee, he has to slurp to avoid spilling.

In two weeks, when school starts, she will quit her job at Downtown Donuts, telling her mother and grandparents only that she needs to spend more time on her school work. High school is way more demanding than junior high. She doesn't tell them about Keefe's comment, or any of the daily ugliness of Downtown Donuts, not because it would surprise or alarm them, but because she did so little. Next time, she tells herself, and she's right about one thing: there will be a next time.

When she stops by Downtown Donuts to give back her uniform and pick up her final paycheck, Leandra is working the front alone. Sophie declines her offer of a freebie dozen. She has tried all the donut varieties, more or less, by then.

"I think I've had enough donuts for a lifetime," she says. "But thanks."

The door behind her opens, and a woman with two blond girls enters, all of them in purple T-shirts, *Missouri Methodist Fellowship* printed in white across the front. Through the door,

Sophie and Leandra watch as people in the same T-shirt stream out of tour bus.

"Duty calls," Leandra says, smiling.

Sophie makes her way out through the throng of purple-shirted people. In the parking lot, she can hear the roar of the interstate, cars speeding past, the eighteen-wheelers and semis hauling livestock or grain, the truckers duty-bound, too.

Though she wasn't in Downtown Donuts long, the smell of the place will cling to her for the rest of the afternoon.

AFTER ALL

IN HER LAST DAYS, when they no longer try to lure her from her narrow bed, she hears singing, lullabies like those her mother sang to her in Ladino or Hebrew, the melodies soft and bright.

"Don't you hear it?" she asks the night nurse, a tall, dark man with the gentlest hands, and improbably, a gold hoop in one ear. A gentle pirate! Or perhaps he's in costume for Purim? Her favorite holiday. But the night nurse—his name escapes her—has taken her temperature and blood pressure and departed, so she cannot ask him. In the morning, she will locate her butterfly costume, the wings she made from wire and muslin and a special, iridescent paint, the cap with its curled antennae. It was her best. She will offer it to her granddaughter Sophie, who should get out more. She's always sitting around here. "Go on," Lise will tell her, handing over the shimmering costume. "Dance."

When her daughter comes the singing is louder, the words more clear, as if a whole choir sings, so she is surprised, then annoyed, when Genny claims not to hear any singing at all.

"Listen," Lise says. "They are so lovely."

"Is there ringing in your ears? Should I get the doctor?"

"Never mind." Lise loves this girl, but they will never see eye to eye. She is too tired to argue with her. She shuts her eyes, hums along with the music.

LATER WHEN SHE AWAKES to supper, Genny is gone, but Esther is here. Lise's heart beats too fast as it always does near Esther, impatient, quick-moving Esther. It's been a long time since Lise has seen her, and still the nervousness. Why after all this time? Should she say something, apologize for taking what wasn't hers? But the child needed her, and Lise went to her, kept her from harm. What else could she have done? What more? True, she needed the child, wanted her. Isn't that, perhaps, a happy consequence of so much sadness?

She thinks to ask Esther, and clears her throat, but the woman before her isn't Esther, after all. It's Sophie, who looks like Esther, with her thin, freckled nose and pale eyes, but is in fact, soft and kind. Sophie bends to kiss her on both cheeks. Relief floods Lise's veins. "I hear the most lovely singing," she says.

"What kind?" Sophie asks.

"*Écoute,*" Lise says. "This one is about a boat on the blue-gray sea."

Sophie takes her hand. "Nice," she says.

"You look like her, but your temperament is more like me," Lise says.

"Like who?" Sophie says.

Lise would like to answer, to tell her more, but her thoughts are like bread thrown to ducks, crumbling, soggy; they sink. She squeezes Sophie's hand to tell her everything she can't say. In her hand, the girl's is slim and cool.

THE SHARP SMELL OF bleach fills the room, though there are undertones of hair in need of washing, and the cafeteria down the hall. The cooking aromas here are nothing like the chicken broth and browning onion smell of Lise's kitchen, but even those would be hard for Sophie to bear right now. She would like to open a window for some fresh air, but she doesn't want to let go of Lise's hand, to disturb her.

The doctor has told them that Lise's heart is slowing. Any day now, he says, but Lise seems unchanged from the previous day. Sophie thinks of Lise's stories of the war, of all the abrupt departures, the hasty gathering of possessions and the abandoning of others and of plans newly laid, seeds sown: *In the summer, we would have carrots and beans.* Now, Lise won't be rushed, won't cooperate with Dr. Shearer's timetable or itinerary. She's taking her sweet time.

Lise murmurs something, too faint for Sophie to make out. In sleep, her face is without guile, childlike despite the deep creases and lines of her skin. Her hair, cut short like a boy's, is white, but threaded through with hints of its previous auburn.

Sitting here, Lise asleep, gives Sophie time to think. She does the math again, counts back. Finn left a month ago, back to Denmark where he will write up the research he conducted here in the University's agronomy fields and lab. She is, according to her calculations, about eight-weeks pregnant. From their time together, Sophie has a series of photos taken at a booth at the Boone County Fair. In one, she and Finn eat cotton candy. In the next shot, they stick out their bright red tongues. The next captures them with open mouths, laughing. In the last, they kiss. They have no plans together beyond this fair, these sugared moments.

There is a knock on the door, and then without a pause, Dr. Shearer appears. "How is she this evening?" he asks.

"The same, I think," Sophie says.

Lise opens her eyes and then shuts them immediately when she sees it's the doctor. It's hard not to read into this Lise's disregard for doctors. She has always preferred home remedies—

charcoal tablets and rice water for stomach upset, a tincture of Valerian for nerves, a cool cloth and a dark room for headaches. And if anyone suggests these methods aren't legitimate, she only laughs and mentions her age. For Sophie's nausea, she would recommend chamomile tea.

"Her body temperature is very low." Dr. Shearer says, and then quietly: "It won't be long now."

Sophie understands that he might be correct, but it's impossible to absorb. Lise dying? He doesn't know who he's talking about. Last year, when Sophie was away on a buying trip for her shop, Genny called to say she should come home right away; Lise was dying. When Sophie got to The Pines, there was Lise, sitting up in the dining hall eating ice cream with a little wooden spoon. It was vanilla, and Lise had pointed out that in general she preferred chocolate.

"She's done this before," Sophie says.

"Still," he says, "you will want to notify your family." And then looking down at Lise's paperwork on his clipboard, "Your rabbi."

How nice it would be to have a guide through this, if not a rabbi then someone wise and calm, to lead the way, and tell them how to behave, what to expect. What they need is a tour guide, someone who will slowly and carefully translate, deliver dates and names, all manner of important facts.

"We're all here," Sophie tells him. "There's no one else." But she decides then that she will have the child. Lise, she believes, would approve. And hadn't Finn's accent reminded her of Jean? Theirs had been a short, happy romance, because both knew it could only be that. Their lives are in different places. Hers here and his in Copenhagen. When she spoke of Finn to Genny or Lise, she called him "my visiting scholar."

LISE WAKES THINKING SHE must post a letter home. She will feel settled only after the letter is in the blue gullet of the mailbox. Instead of *mailbox* she thinks *pelican*. She knows this is the wrong word but being wrong isn't so very troubling. Perhaps where she is going (this is the first time that she understands that she is again embarking on a journey) one can be wrong with impunity. Correct or incorrect, it hardly matters.

Despite what Genny thinks, the singing continues, fainter as if the singers are growing weary. She wishes Genny would try to hear them. But Genny is strong willed, like her mother. She is thinking of Esther, not herself, but she laughs then, because *she* is Genny's mother, after all.

"What is it, Mother?" Genny asks.

Lise reaches for her hand. "Eh, *voilà*," she says.

FUNNY, SHE DOESN'T RECALL stepping onto the train. There has been no particular fuss about tickets or identity papers. She doesn't have any luggage beside her, no parcels. Maybe the bags are in the rack above or stowed in a compartment at the end of this car. Or perhaps she is traveling light as she has certainly done before. The train heaves into motion then, and Lise settles back in her seat. The movement makes her drowsy, like being rocked in a cradle. She thinks of Eugénie—or was it Sophie?—as a baby, fussing and tired, but fighting sleep, unwilling to miss a thing. Her eyes would droop closed and then snap open, outraged that she'd been fooled into calm.

The train passes clusters of houses with tile roofs, then pastures and orchards. It winds through woods where Lise spots deer, their big eyes unblinking. How inviting the forest is, dappled with sunlight, ferns swaying by the stream. Velvet moss covers the stones. Her heart feels funny for a moment, fluttery, but then it stills. The train leaves the woods and moves through open ground. For a short while there is nothing, and then the train cuts through lush fields of bright green. With pleasure, Lise recalls this color's name: *chartreuse.*

From the porch of an old farmhouse, a little boy with a red wagon loaded with firewood waves to her, his wave a benediction and a promise—of what, she doesn't know. She would like to brush back his thick bangs. She has secrets to whisper into the pink shell of his ear. At the very least she would like to wave back to him, but the train has sped up and passed him and his fields, the big chapped farmhouse.

The boy is gone. Gone, like so much else. *Oh, well,* she thinks, *another time.* She sinks back into her seat, closes her eyes. If she is very still, she can just make out the singing. The voices lull her. How easy it is, after all, this leaving. After all.

IN MEMORIAM

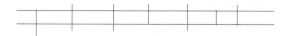

GENNY KNEW, OF COURSE, that living on a main thoroughfare would present certain problems, but the house was perfect for her—white clapboard with red shutters, a tidy garden, the small room off the kitchen with built-in bookshelves for her study. And after a month here, she's mostly grown accustomed to the sounds of cars and trucks at all hours, their clanking mufflers and loud music and honking. At night after the student bars close, she hears the students coming home—shouting or laughing—or once singing that old song "To Sir With Love."

The noise, which she's come to think of as hubbub, is tolerable, but what is no longer tolerable is *the shrine*. When had she started calling it that? Perhaps someone else said it first, a colleague, maybe, joking about the bad taste of it: "Hey, how's your shrine?" Not only is it ugly, it's directly in front of her house, on the maple tree in the parkway: plastic flowers, once pink and yellow, now gray with road grime, the photos of the dead man, a gold plastic cross, stuffed animals tacked up in plastic bags. By the foot of the tree, the mourners have left beer cans. Occasionally there are empty wine or liquor bottles. Enough already, she thinks. It's been more than a year according to the obituary laminated and tacked to the tree.

When she first considered buying this house, she hadn't noticed the shrine, which seems impossible to her now. She'd been charmed by the flagstone path, the cozy rooms, and good light. She'd been ready for a fresh start.

Now settled in, she's supposed to be writing a paper for the annual French-literature conference she will attend next month in Chicago, a paper on Voltaire's *Candide*. Instead of writing, though, she's thinking about the tree and the dead man, a boy really—just twenty-one. From the window in her study, she can see all the photos tacked to the trunk. Online, she can't find an article about the accident, only his obituary which is already posted on the tree. "Survived by his wife, Sara." In the phone book there are several S. Caswells, all on the south side of town. She writes the numbers and addresses down for later, though she can't imagine calling. What would she say? What does one say? Her armpits and the back of her knees are damp. She can't concentrate here. She'll go to the library to work, she decides, away from the tree and its gaudy display of loss, but she sets a deadline. The shrine will be down by her granddaughter's birthday party in a month. She and Sophie, her daughter, have planned to have it on the porch—just a few friends and cake for Mia, who will turn two, wine and cheese for the adults. Genny intends to have the planters filled by then and her window boxes—everything overflowing with color and glossy leaves.

Leaving her house, she sees that the plastic bags containing the stuffed animals are slipping, their corners heavy with condensation. They are suffocating, Genny thinks, and her own breath comes out in a wispy sigh.

Only weeks ago, the lawns were yellow, the trees bare, but now everything is new-green. The finches dart after each other, filled with bird desire. They seem not to care about anything else—humans in their path, cars, houses. Students are out in droves, walking or biking, giddy with the new warmth. Car windows are rolled down and as the cars pass, Genny hears a mosaic of music and news. Before long it will be soupy hot here; the only sign of life, the drone of air conditioners. It's pretty out, it is, but Genny can't help feeling that time has sped up, a mean trick. It's been almost a year since her mastectomy, an anniversary she mentions to no one.

How did he die? she wonders. Asleep at the wheel? Drunk? A heart attack?

THAT NIGHT, SHE HEARS their cars and trucks stop outside, hears gravel crunching beneath their feet as they move to the tree. From the living-room window, she watches them, drinking from a tall bottle they pass around. There are five or six guys, a girl with long brown braids, and another girl with who sits cross-legged on the sidewalk. The tallest guy lights a candle, and they bow their heads. Outside, the mourners have their arms around each other, and they sway as if to music. Genny can't hear any, though.

By two in the morning, they are gone, but Genny can't sleep. When she lies down, her mind fills with thoughts: Who was this guy, Shawn Caswell, so loved by his friends, she wonders. Genny has no graves to visit, to tend here, not even for Lise and Jean, who donated their bodies to science. And she is fading; she feels this at night—always at night—the cancer finding her.

"MOM?" SOPHIE SAYS. "ARE you OK?"

Genny sits up on the couch, shakes her head. A copy of *Candide* is open on her chest. "What time is it?" She's been dreaming that she was lost. In her dream, the streets were narrow and twisting. The sun blazed overhead.

"About four. Are you sick?" Sophie is wearing a bowling shirt from the fifties with the name *Louie* stitched on the pocket.

"No, I'm not sick, Sophie." This comes out with more bite than she intends. More gently she adds: "I was up late last night watching them out there at my tree."

"What do you mean?" Sophie plops down on the couch, slips her clogs off. She has come from the vintage clothing store she owns, Frocks, and she smells vaguely of mothballs and patchouli.

"The friends of that guy who died come at night sometimes. They stand around drinking and talking. Sometimes they light candles."

"Did they see you watching?"

"I don't think so." She doesn't tell Sophie that she plans to talk with them next time.

Sophie pulls back the living-room curtains to see the tree. Several beer cans are scattered around the base of the tree. "I read somewhere that the dead are supposed to be very thirsty," Sophie says.

"It's ugly," Genny says.

"Don't you think there's something kind of touching about it?" Sophie says. "I've seen these memorials on the highway too—attached to mile markers or telephone poles."

It's just like Sophie to take the other side, she thinks. "I shouldn't have to see all that junk every time I look outside." She knows suddenly what part of the shrine she hates the most—not the dismal plastic flowers or the pathetic notes and photos, not even the beer cans or bottles; it's the extravagance of their grief. This is what grates on her.

Sophie is looking at her with the expression she uses with Mia, a look of willed patience, as if Genny must be humored.

"Look," Sophie says, "I've got to get Mia at daycare. I just stopped by to see if you want to join us for an early supper and a walk?"

172

"I hate to pass up any time with Mia, but I've got this paper to write.

"Good luck," Sophie says.

"I can't remember why I thought there was anything more to say about *Candide*."

"You'll think of something," Sophie says.

"Kiss Mia for me," Genny calls from the porch. As Sophie backs out of the driveway, one of the beer cans rolls from under the tree. It clanks back and forth by the curb and then blows into a pile of leaves and rubbish. That's what we need, Genny thinks, a big wind, and she imagines a tornado, like a giant vacuum cleaner, sucking up all the junk.

She moves around the kitchen making a salad for her dinner. She'll eat on the porch and then get to work on the paper. *Pluck*, Genny thinks. This is how she would like to be remembered. *A person with pluck*. Why is she thinking this now? The tree. It's making her morbid. Morbid and distracted; she has oversalted her salad. She eats it anyway, going over her notes.

THERE MUST BE A drink special at Moody's. All night Genny can hear the pedestrians loud and silly outside. She is prepared for the mourners with a six-pack of Budweiser she bought this afternoon. She drinks from a can, small tentative sips. She'd rather have a glass of Merlot, but that won't do. It's essential that they drink the same thing together.

The thump of bass is the most noticeable in the precise moment the music is turned off, in the sudden shocking quiet that emerges. How do they speak or even think in their cars and trucks, Genny wonders. This is not a good conversation starter, she understands. She waits until she hears the truck doors open and slam shut. Another car pulls up. Genny hears voices, doors creaking. Cigarette smoke wafts in the kitchen window.

She takes the six-pack in one hand and her half-full can in the other and stops on the porch to watch. The mourners have gathered in a small circle next to the tree, their hands in their pockets and their heads bowed. Genny hesitates at the threshold of her door. The night air feels soft against her face as she descends her porch steps. Her motion-sensor light flashes on and the group turns and looks at her.

"Yo," the tallest guy says.

"Hello," Genny says. "Nice night, huh?"

"Yeah."

"Not bad."

"Beer?" Genny says, swinging the beer forward.

No one responds. "Have a beer?" she repeats.

"Dude, thanks," the tallest guys says. He takes the beer and expertly extracts a can, passes the rest. Hands come out of pockets.

Genny drinks from her can. Warm, the beer tastes metallic, but it gives her something to do, a chance to look at the mourners. They are younger than she thought, boys more than men, sweet-cheeked beneath their bad haircuts. They are thinner, too, without their parkas and layers.

"He was your friend?" she says.

"Yeah," says the boy to her right, lifting his beer can as if to toast. "He was the best."

On his bicep, he has a tattoo, an intricately detailed rose twisting around a dagger. The tattoo strikes her as strangely pretty. The petals ripple as the arm is thrust out to her. "I'm Cyril," he says. "This is Mitch, Tyson, Derrick, and Sonny."

"Pleased to meet you," Genny says and introduces herself.

"You live here?" Tyson says. His eyes are rimmed in thick lashes.

"Yes, I do," Genny says. "What about you all—where do you live?"

They name streets south of town.

"Shawn, too?" Genny asks, afraid for the first time as she says his name aloud.

"Yeah," Mitch says. "We're buds our whole lives."

No one corrects the verb tense. "What was he like?" Genny asks.

"He'd take a bullet for us," Derrick says.

"He was like a brother to me," Tyson says, wiping at his eyes, his long lashes webbed with tears.

"You all made this memorial to him?" Her voice comes out fractured, wobbly.

"Yeah, some other people, too," Cyril says, kicking at the ground.

"He was like a fucking brother to us all," Mitch says, crushing his beer can in his fist. Another can materializes—from his jacket pocket? A backpack? Thin air? Genny doesn't know.

"Is there also a gravesite?" Genny asks. She sees a car slowing as it approaches.

"Yeah, but this is the place, you know? The place he left us."

"Fucking here, man."

"They say everything happens for a reason, but I don't know," Mitch says.

"I don't believe that, either," Genny says. And while she is watching the boys, she's thinking, too, of her paper, of how that phrase—everything happens for a reason—is exactly what Voltiare rejected more than 200 years ago. She feels heartened by this agreement with the mourners, this understanding.

The car—a Volvo with parking stickers from the college—pulls up by the tree. It's her colleague Jerome and his partner, Miles. "Genny?" Jerome calls. "Everything OK, darling?"

"Fine," Genny says, waving them on.

The mourners have taken in the expensive car, the stickers, Jerome's accent, the sultry jazz wafting out the window.

"Sorry," Genny says, unsure what she is apologizing for.

Nobody speaks. Genny watches Jerome's car take a left onto College Avenue. At their house they'll sip Cointreau on the porch, she imagines, talk about the trip they're planning to see Jerome's family in Marseille or about Miles' novel.

She forges ahead: "Now that it's spring, maybe we could plant some real flowers here, make a bed around the tree." She speaks quickly or she might not finish. "I could buy the plants. Maybe some of those blue flowers called forget-me-nots? They would do well here."

Genny watches as the wind lifts the plastic flowers on the tree. The bags rustle.

"Cool," Mitch says.

"Dude, don't you get it?" Derrick says. "She wants the stuff to come down."

"No way?" Mitch says.

"Is that what you mean?" Cyril says, squinting.

"I don't want to take your memorial away—it's not that."

"Yes, you do. That's exactly what you want."

"This is city property," Cyril says. "It's ours just as much as it's yours."

"We don't need you to buy us flowers. We got flowers," Tyson says, tapping the plastic lilies tacked above the picture of Shawn.

"There are ordinances," Genny says, "rules about posting, and littering." She isn't even sure this is true, but her voice sounds certain, professorial. "I thought we could work something out."

The clock tower on campus rings two times. "It's late," she says. "Will you think about my offer?" It is quiet as she turns and mounts her steps. Inside, behind the locked door, Genny feels her heart banging inside her chest. She has to lean against the wall to steady her breath.

SHE SHOULD BE WRITING. She leaves for Chicago next week and her paper is still unfinished, so why is she driving south, past campus, past the Sav-U-More and Big Lots toward the address she believes to be the home of Shawn Caswell's widow? Such a formidable word: widow. A word demanding respect, unlike the words that might be applied to Genny: *divorcée*, or *orphan*, which elicit pity more than respect. Or *survivor*, a word she can't bear for its too-close relation to victim. She doesn't want any of those labels.

The road she is on forks without warning or signs, and Genny finds herself entering a trailer park: Ferguson Estates. Leggy pansies and clumps of spikey grass bloom from old tires painted white, and there are street signs again. She locates June Road and follows it until it dead ends by a cornfield. Here is the Caswell home. Set back in a muddy lot, it looks tossed there—an empty cigarette carton. The front windows are propped open, screenless, and the blue curtains are knotted instead of tied back. As she nears the trailer, she smells stale cigarette smoke. On the porch, which she ascends carefully, there is a chair splintered in half and an empty recycling bin. From inside, she hears nothing. She knocks on the door and waits. If no one is home, Genny can leave a note, but what would she write?

The door opens as Genny is considering. The widow Caswell, as Genny has come to think of her, is small and blond and pink-skinned in her flowered nightgown.

"I've awakened you," Genny says. "I'm sorry."

The girl looks at her blandly, neither contradicting nor offering apologies of her own. It is two in the afternoon, after all, Genny thinks.

The girl's gaze moves beyond Genny to her car parked in front. "You need some hauling done?" she asks.

"Excuse me?"

"If you're looking for Shawn to do some hauling, he's dead," the girl says. She pushes her blond hair behind her ear and Genny sees a purplish bruise on her neck.

"No," Genny says. "I know he died and I'm sorry."

The girl scratches absently at her bare arm.

"I wanted to talk with you about the memorial for Shawn on College Street. I just moved into the house—and well, it's my tree."

"Who's there?" The male voice is thick with sleep.

It's Tyson, Genny sees when he gets closer. He is shirtless, his chest hairless except for a thin trail of black below his navel. "I'll handle this," he says to Sara, who turns and recedes into the darkness of the trailer. Genny hears what sounds like a cat, though perhaps it is a baby.

"She's been through enough without you coming here."

"I know," Genny starts.

"No, you don't know. You don't know shit." He pushes open the screen door and steps onto the porch.

Genny knows how grief can make you behave strangely, unpredictably. She should be scared. No one knows she's come here. But the look on Tyson's face is sheepish, not angry. He feels caught, found out. His buddies don't know he sleeps here with his dead friend's wife. The maroon splotch on Sara's neck is from him, a hickey, Sophie used to call them. Tyson and Sara are moving on, doing what people say one should. In other circumstances, Genny might mention that some cultures view it as the brother's duty to step in and marry the widow. Isn't that what Tyson called Shawn—his brother?

"I'll take care of your fucking tree," he says hugging himself as if modest or cold. "Just back off, OK?"

178

Back in her car, she finds she is shaking. She'd like to tell Tyson and the girl that she knows a thing or two about loss, but what good would that do?

MAYBE TYSON TELLS THE others that Sara wants it down. Maybe he says it's time to move on. Possibly they believed Genny about the ordinance. Or maybe Sara says what people often say of the dead: "He would want us to." Genny expected she'd hear them, but the shrine disappears silently in the night. When Genny takes her coffee onto the porch, she sees the naked tree. Nothing remains of the wreaths or the flowers, not even a scrap of the posters, only an off-brand vodka bottle propped against the knobby roots. When it is retrieved and deposited in her recycling bin by the back gate, the tree is hers again. She makes a note to buy the forget-me-nots when she gets back from Chicago.

MIA'S PARTY GOES OFF without a hitch. No one, not even Sophie, mentions the shrine or its absence. Mia loves her presents and the cake, and Sophie lets her eat two pieces while the adults drink wine and eat the Brie and baguette Genny has bought, the Greek olives from the crackled glass dish. Genny plays with Mia and her new wooden puzzle in a sunny spot on the front lawn. Her friends talk and laugh, help themselves to more wine.

"Did you notice it's gone," she says to Thérèse, her friend from the history department. She gestures toward the tree. Yes, it was Thérèse who first called it Genny's shrine.

"I see," says Thérèse. "Much better."

"I've got to get this one home," Sophie says joining them with Mia in her arms.

"Did you notice?" Genny asks. She has been wanting to talk about this all afternoon, she realizes.

"It's gone," Sophie says. "Are you happy now?"

Genny looks away, down College. It is strangely quiet. "You have to admit, it looks a lot better," she says.

Mia squawks, and Sophie hands her to Genny, so she can gather up the mess of presents, paper, bows, and boxes. "You're getting so big," Genny tells her. "Two years old!" She nuzzles Mia's neck, which makes her squirm and giggle.

LATER IT WILL SEEM as if she were there, not in Chicago speaking of *Candide* and the tenacity of Pangloss' philosophy. So vividly can she imagine the roar of the saws, their sharp teeth, the men in hardhats and work boots, the shouted orders. In her mind, she transposes the events: the removal of the shrine and the removal of the tree, so that it is cut down in the dark, but of course it couldn't have happened that way. In telling the story, she will forget to mention that the old tree was a nuisance. Each week something fell from it—helicopters which sprouted madly, fuzzy wormy things, a yellow-green pollen which made her sneeze and coated her car windows. She should be glad it's gone, shouldn't she? The whole thing wiped clean, a fresh start. The city produces a sapling in a burlap bag almost immediately, and a team of men who plant and stake it. The letter from the city she failed to read explains that her tree—a Norway maple— was infected with a virus that shrivels the leaves and marks them with black splotches. It was just a tree, she might tell herself later, but when she first sees it gone, she can only rock back and forth on the parkway, her cries twisting into the sounds of traffic.

IN THE CEMETERIES OF SAINT-MALO

THE NUMBERS OCCUPY HER as she walks. At 58, Genny is more than twice the age her mother was when she died. Her daughter, Sophie, is in fact, older now than Genny's mother was when she died. And this odd bit of math: her granddaughter is older already than Genny was when she lost her mother. Genny is tired from the travel—the long plane ride, the delays in New York, the crowded train from Paris, so her mind keeps snagging on these facts as if the numbers might compute differently and yield something new. She has come to France this summer to direct a study-abroad program and has arrived a week early to see the place where her mother is buried. Though she has been to France many times—the summer program is popular, and Genny is the department's best-liked professor—she has never returned to Saint-Malo. And even now, she doesn't completely trust her impulse to come. What does she think she will find?

The cobblestone streets and the stone buildings look familiar, she thinks as she walks, though she can't possibly remember Saint-Malo. She was not quite two when she left. Could it be that it looks like other French towns she has visited? Now before her, she sees a nun leading a line of uniformed little girls into the Cathédrale St. Vincent. One girl has the same soft curls as

Mia. Without meaning to, she enters the *cathédrale* behind the girls, watches as they file into the pews. It is cool inside and Genny buttons her sweater. As if choreographed, the girls kneel and cross themselves. Genny feels a pinch of envy, but for what? She takes in the stained-glass windows, the case of relics by the entry. On her way out, she passes a row of dark confessionals. In one, below the velvet curtain, she sees a woman's swollen ankles and feet crammed into high-heeled pumps. On her own feet, Genny wears comfortable walking shoes, their laces double-knotted, though she knows the shoes mark her as an American.

Outside the *cathédrale*, her eyes take a moment to readjust to the daylight. Overhead gulls squawk and trill. Genny can smell the sea, too, though she hasn't yet seen it. It is not far now to her first destination.

In the Syndicat d'Initiative, she is taken to the bureau of tourism. The man behind the desk introduces himself as Monsieur Dufour and invites her to sit. He is wearing the nicest suit she has ever seen, of a material so supple she wants to reach out and touch it.

"What may I do for you?" he asks in English.

In French, Genny explains what she wants. There is a slight, nearly imperceptible change in Monsieur Dufour's face when he hears her French. She continues, withdrawing the death certificate from her purse. She knows the date of her mother's death: May 1940. What she would like to know is where her mother, a Jew, might be buried.

Monsieur Dufour sighs. "Those were bad times," he says. "A pity, Madame Horton, and matters got worse before they got better."

He is about her age, Genny thinks, maybe a little older. If things had been different they might have been schoolmates.

"The records, Madame, are kept at the cemeteries. There are three that were in use at that time, all with a Jewish section."

182

He writes the names of the cemeteries on a piece of paper and hands it to Genny. "This one, you are not far from now. The others are farther away."

"*Merci, Monsieur,*" Genny says rising. "You have been very helpful."

"I hope you will take in the other sights while you are here—the beaches are some of the most beautiful in Europe, the rampart walkways, Île Cézembre, just a short boat ride away. Lovely—and there is a legend about it involving a three-tailed lizard that you will find interesting."

Genny thanks him again, relieved he doesn't ply her with the glossy pamphlets displayed by the door. She departs, her sensible shoes squeaking over the marble floor. In France, everyone is a historian, she thinks. In the states, the past is the past. Her students don't remember Chernobyl, to them the Gulf War was about T-shirts emblazoned with the American flag. The Jews in Israel have only ever been the oppressor. And where is she on this spectrum? Her run-in with history has left her knowledgeable, but like most Americans, she finds the past a bulky, inconvenient thing. And the present keeps getting shorter, faster, like a train she must run to catch. She doesn't like to think back to her illness just two years ago.

The cemetery is only a five-minute walk from the mayor's office. It is under tall, old trees, on top of a hill. The wrought-iron fence surrounding it buckles in places, sways out in others, but inside the fence it is tidy, well kept. The graves are close together with less ornamentation than she is accustomed to. After the war and the confirmation of her father's death, Genny's aunt and uncle adopted her and took her with them to America. Why they settled in Daly City, California, a city known for its number of cemeteries, Genny will never know. Did they think she was already immunized against death? She was just a girl and had lost both her parents.

In the Cimetière Saint-Malo, Genny walks the rows until she comes to the Jewish section, recognizable from a distance by the rocks lining the grave markers. Here she stops to read the stones. René Rubin, b. 1916, d. 1957, Natalie Bouchard, b. 1937—the year Genny was born—d. 1987. Genny tightens her sweater around herself. By Natalie's grave, maroon and yellow pansies grow. She moves on to a row of smaller markers, worn smooth from years in the salt air. Genny cannot make out the names. Perhaps one of these is her mother, she thinks. What will she do if she finds her mother's grave here? She isn't the type to fall prostrate on the grave, weeping and moaning, can't see herself having a conversation with a mother she can't remember. Even if she'd brought flowers to plant, who would care for them when she left? So far, Genny has thought only as far as the search.

At the caretaker's building, she raps on the door. It's opened by a young man with ruddy cheeks. She expected someone older, grizzled. This is not a job for the young, she thinks.

"*Bonjour, Monsieur,*" she begins. "I am looking for a particular grave."

Nodding slightly, the man beckons her in, motions to a chair. He sits behind a desk and writes something on a pad, then extends it to her.

"*Je suis sourd,*" she reads.

He is deaf. His youth in this place makes sense to her now. He can't hear the gravedigger's shovels hitting the rocky soil, the mourners crying. On the pad, she writes her request. She fishes the death certificate out of her purse and passes it over with the pad. He takes both and leaves the room. When he returns, he is carrying a black ledger. The binding says 1939-40. As he opens it, the binding makes a cracking noise and Genny smells musty dampness.

He motions for her to look with him. The pages are filled with the cramped, dark handwriting of another generation. It is hard to decipher, but it appears the deaths are listed by date. In May of 1940, 23 people were buried here, but not her mother. She double checks, even flipping ahead to September.

On the pad, she writes *"Elle n'est pas ici. Merci."*

The man nods again, seems to shrug his shoulders, though perhaps he is only stretching. Outside the gate, Genny crosses Cimetière Saint-Malo off her list.

Walking again, she understands why this place looks so familiar. The streets and houses, the fountains and sunny squares, she knows from Lise's paintings. She thinks of one in particular—a street scene in the plums and blues of dawn, a kerchiefed woman, her head bent, as she makes her way home.

BY THE TIME SHE reaches the second cemetery, the sun is high in the sky. She is tired, feeling the effects of her travel, the heat. Here, there are fewer trees and many of the flowers are plastic. The real ones look parched and browned at their edges. Again she walks to the caretaker's building and explains her situation. When she is done, the caretaker rises to retrieve the record books. He is gone a long time and his office smells of his lunch. When he returns with the records, Genny sees it is the same kind of big book as the first cemetery—heavy and black, the years inscribed on its spine.

"Merci," she says, taking the book.

"Vous êtes Belge?" the caretaker asks.

And she is forced to explain her past. Her mother's death, her father's death, the move to America.

"You have a small accent," he says, "but other than that your French is very good."

This happens often when she comes to France. All those years of speaking French only with Lise and Jean have altered her French, tinged it with something no one can quite place. It's a dialect of three, their own patois. A wave of longing for them passes through her. A dialect of one.

"I have a cousin in America," the caretaker says. "In Philadelphia."

"A lovely city," Genny says, before opening the ledger. This cemetery must be bigger, because in May 1940 almost fifty people were buried here, but not her mother.

"These records are absolutely complete?"

"*Bien sûr,*" he says. "I wish you well on your search."

Genny thanks him, crossing this cemetery from her list. She's starting to feel as if the excursion to Saint-Malo has been a mistake. She'll be worn out when her students arrive in Paris with their homesickness and missing luggage, their loud talk, talk, talk. She'll need all her wits then. How foolish to come here hoping to meet up with her past. The past is gone. She of all people should know that. If she were not suddenly so tired, she could leave for Paris immediately.

She will find a place to eat and then proceed. She moves toward the walled city, passing buttery stucco buildings, window boxes exploding with geraniums. The restaurant she decides on opens out to a small courtyard. Tables surround a fountain, its insides coated with a velvety moss. Genny orders the prix fixe—pâté with cornichons, coq au vin, and a salad with vinaigrette—which comes with a half carafe of wine. She is glad to sit down in the cool courtyard, glad the French are used to lone diners. At another table an elderly gentleman eats and reads a newspaper, his dog curled by his feet. But it is nice later when the man and a woman at the next table turn to her and introduce themselves. They have noticed her guidebook on the table and assume she is American.

Their names are Matthias and Beata. They are here from Hamburg to celebrate twenty years of marriage. Beata's smile is broad and welcoming, but her eyes keep blinking as if she has something in them—an eyelash or a bit of dirt. Matthias's well-trimmed beard is peppered with gray.

"Congratulations," Genny says. Some quick calculations and she decides they must be in their mid-forties. Younger than she, too young to have known the war in which she was the enemy, but what of their parents and grandparents? It seems rude to think this in the face of their friendliness. They have even offered her a glass of wine from their carafe.

"Please," Beata says, "and bring your chair around." She wears a blue-green scarf, a deep, lonesome color, which Lise used often in painting the sea or shadows. The blue-green is called viridian, Genny recalls. Funny, that she has thought of this trip as a search for Esther, but everywhere she turns, it is Lise who comes to mind.

Matthias, it turns out, is a professor of animal husbandry and has been to Missouri, to the very university where Genny teaches—it is known for its agriculture programs and its practical sciences. Beata is a librarian, and they are parents of two sons—twelve and eighteen. Beata takes a photo from her purse to show Genny. In the picture the two boys wear bright-colored parkas and stand next to each other on a ski slope.

"Fine-looking boys," Genny says.

"And you?"

"Yes, a daughter, Sophie. The only pictures I have of her are old ones, school pictures, but here is my granddaughter." She hands Mia's picture across the table.

Their response is what Genny has come to expect: "She looks like you," Beata says.

It is true, though Mia is blond and blue-eyed and Genny has dark hair, dark eyes. She can't say what features are hers on her granddaughter's face, but when she looks at Mia she has the feeling she has seen her somewhere before.

"We look forward to being grandparents one day," Matthias says. "How lucky you are."

Genny remembers something someone said at a cancer-survivor group when Genny had mentioned her mastectomy discomfort. "I just feel lucky," the woman had said, "that I can hold my grandbaby and watch him grow up." Yes, Genny thought, but what of the purplish scar across your chest? The body's ridiculous asymmetry? Why is it that the unlucky are always the first to speak of luck?

"What brings you to Saint-Malo?" Matthias asks.

What he means, Genny thinks, is what has brought her to Saint-Malo alone. Its attractions are obvious for family vacations, romantic getaways. She intends to tell them about the study-abroad program, but she finds herself (is it the wine?) telling them of her search.

"So you are French then?" Matthias says.

"Yes and no. I became American."

"I see," he says.

Genny is even more surprised to hear herself say, "I had breast cancer." This is something she rarely talks about with anyone, let alone new acquaintances. What has she done? She waits for the awkward silence, or worse the pitying looks and loud, syrupy exclamations of regret.

"I, too," says Beata. "Two years ago."

This is so unexpected, Genny thinks she might laugh—or cry. "I am sorry," she says instead. "Are you well now?"

"We hope," Beata says, shrugging. Her eyes blink more rapidly.

Does something about Beata's brush with death show on her? Is this what prompted Genny's confession? Maybe you can't take away a woman's breast and expect her to go unchanged elsewhere—her eyes, the set of her mouth, her posture as she ventures out in the world. "Your scarf," Genny says, "I keep admiring it."

"I just bought it today—on rue de Dinan. A local artist. Here," she says, pulling a card from the outer pocket of her backpack.

The talk turns then to treatments and doctors, to remission and soy. By now it is getting late. The waiter has long ago cleared their plates, and glasses. He glowers by the courtyard doors.

"I should get back to my search," Genny says.

They exchange addresses. Matthias will perhaps come back to Missouri, and Beata encourages Genny to visit Germany.

"Good luck!" they call down the cobbled street. "Good-bye."

THE LAST CEMETERY ON her list is inside the walled city. It is small and dark, in the shadows of the wall. The caretaker's building is by the front gates, and Genny goes there directly. Again she knocks on the door, prepares to explain herself. The door is opened by a middle-aged woman in a flowered housedress.

"Come in, come in," she says. "You have caught me on my way out of town. How fortunate, *non?* Even in an hour, there would be no one here."

She listens as Genny explains what she is looking for. Then she rises and goes to shelves which Genny hadn't noticed as she entered. She takes a book from the top shelf.

"This is the year our records begin—again you are fortunate. You look for May?"

"Yes."

"*Et voilà,*" the caretaker says, handing the book to Genny.

The printing is very small, and the light is poor, but she must be here, Genny thinks. There is nowhere else to look. On the second page, Genny's finger rests on her mother's name: Esther Dondich, age 27, *épouse de* Alain Latour, row 13, square

F. What does she know of this woman? She has seen a few old photographs. In each her mother looks different—thin and pensive in one, plump in another, unreadable in yet another. Genny has her mother's passport, which lists the place of her birth as Latvia and gives the names of her parents, people long dead. She has Lise's stories, but they are imprecise like the photos, and even grainier, as if overexposed.

"Come, I will show you where she was," the caretaker says.

"Was?" Genny asks.

"Naturally . . . I thought you would know." She stops. "I am sorry, Madame. This is a small cemetery in a small country, not like America."

"Excuse me?" Genny says. The caretaker's words are not adding up for her.

"Regularly it becomes necessary for us to make room. The coffins are dug up and the remains disposed of. You can see we are crowded to the rafters as it is, and people do not stop dying."

Grusome images come to her, photographs of corpses stacked in front of barracks, piles of human bones buried in pits. She knows this is different, but she can't shake those images, the horrible disregard.

"Would you be interested in seeing the plot?" the woman asks. She is trying, Genny sees; this isn't her policy after all, but Genny can't look at her.

"I will find it, thank you."

"Very well," the woman says, turning. Genny can hear the gravel crunching under foot as the caretaker makes her way to her office.

Genny finds row thirteen and moves sideways from there until she reaches the seventh gravestone. The plot is occupied now by Sabine Samuelson, who lived to the ripe old age of ninety-three. There are several small stones on the marker, left by mourners to show they haven't forgotten Sabine. And the plot itself looks like any other. Did she attend her mother's burial, Genny wonders. There are no memories, not a single one, just black space. And how did Lise explain her mother's sudden absence? There is no one left for Genny to ask. She thinks of the story Lise loved to tell of coming to collect Genny when Esther was dying and Alain was stationed at the Maginot Line and how the child Genny reached up to her and said, "Maman!" Genny suspects that there is more to this story, its edges smoothed away from repeated tellings. Jean and Lise loved her, cared for her, found a way to get her eggs and milk all through the war. There were no other children.

What is she doing standing in this graveyard? It seems urgent that she see something else of this town—the beach, the sea. Clutching her purse and her guidebook, Genny walks briskly back to the gate and exits the cemetery. Just past the caretaker's building, she sees the stone ramp leading to the walkway. She moves toward it though it will take her in the opposite direction of her hotel. She is winded when she reaches the top, as if she has been pulling a great weight. She stops to catch her breath. The sea before her is beautiful—gray-green stretching to meet the sky. More of Lise's colors: carmine, cerulean, Antwerp blue.

The beaches are emptying out, though it seems early—only three o'clock. Genny watches as the people fold up their brightly striped chairs and umbrellas. She sees a little boy run squealing and naked for the water and watches as his father scoops him up, scolding. The vendors are no longer hawking their refreshments. They move hurriedly towards the ramparts, pushing their small stainless-steel carts. The sunlight glints off the carts, making Genny squint.

The ramparts are suddenly teeming with people from the beach, sweaty and smiling, carrying big straw bags, umbrellas, armfuls of towels. A young couple kissing nearly walks into her.

She watches the people pass, moving toward the cafés and pubs of the city center. She starts to follow. She can stop at the artist's shop, buy scarves like Beata's, souvenirs, a doll, perhaps, for Mia.

When she looks back out at the sea, the beach is gone. She understands now: it is high tide. She has read in her guidebook about the abrupt tidal shifts here. The water comes in so quickly that each year unsuspecting tourists are drowned. Below her, the dark waves smack against the ramparts as if angry. The beach is gone, completely covered by the waves. Except for a yellow plastic beach toy bobbing up and down, it might not have existed at all.

Watching, Genny Horton, *née* Eugénie Latour, knows what to do. She turns and walks back to the cemetery, back to Esther's long-ago grave. By the gate, she stoops and picks up a small speckled rock. Smooth, it fits in the palm of her hand. In the distance Genny can hear the bleep of a siren.

Luckily, the caretaker's car is gone, so Genny won't have to speak to her again. She couldn't explain herself if she had to, in any language. Genny finds the row, counts over again, and then she is at Madame Samuelson's headstone. The siren is faint now, and the cemetery is still. She places her rock, not on the gravestone, but at the other end, for Esther, her mother, who is not forgotten. There are still unanswered questions, wide gaps in what Genny knows of the past, and so much missing, lost. Her longing won't go away, but there is also this: a small brown stone, warm from the sun, the salt air, the sea in the distance, its passionate waves.

Rachel Hall's short stories and essays have appeared in a number of journals and anthologies, including *Black Warrior Review*, *Crab Orchard Review*, *Gettysburg Review*, *Fifth Wednesday*, and *New Letters*, which awarded her the Alexander Cappon Prize for Fiction. She has received other honors and awards from *Lilith*, *Glimmer Train*, the Bread Loaf Writers' Conference, Ragdale, the Ox-Bow School of the Arts, and the Constance Saltonstall Foundation for the Arts. Hall is a professor of English in the creative writing program at the State University of New York at Geneseo where she holds two Chancellor's Awards for Excellence, for teaching and for creative work. She lives in Rochester, New York, with her husband and daughter. Her family's wartime papers and photographs, the inspiration for these stories, were recently donated to the United States Holocaust Memorial Museum in Washington, DC.

www.rachelhall.org

Previous winners of the
G. S. Sharat Chandra Prize for Short Fiction

A Bed of Nails by Ron Tanner,
selected by Janet Burroway

I'll Never Leave You by H. E. Francis,
selected by Diane Glancy

The Logic of a Rose: Chicago Stories by Billy Lombardo,
selected by Gladys Swan

Necessary Lies by Kerry Neville Bakken,
selected by Hilary Masters

Love Letters from a Fat Man by Naomi Benaron,
selected by Stuart Dybek

Tea and Other Ayama Na Tales by Eleanor Bluestein,
selected by Marly Swick

Dangerous Places by Perry Glasser,
selected by Gary Gildner

Georgic by Mariko Nagai,
selected by Jonis Agee

Living Arrangements by Laura Maylene Walter,
selected by Robert Olen Butler

Garbage Night at the Opera by Valerie Fioravanti,
selected by Jacquelyn Mitchard

Boulevard Women by Lauren Cobb,
selected by Kelly Cherry

Thorn by Evan Morgan Williams,
selected by Al Young

King of the Gypsies by Lenore Myka,
selected by Lorraine M. López